"Someone's tampered with the car," Tyler said.

If so—and the bastard had arrived on the scene before Tyler—Julie would have had more than harmless cattle to crack her whip at.

Julie's first words to him had been to ask why he was following her. He'd taken the question as ludicrous, but for all he knew, some nefarious character had been tailing her.

His apprehension surged when he saw the note attached to the steering wheel. He squinted in the sunlight to make out the words.

In spite of the scribbled print, the message was clear.

Someone wanted Julie out of Mustang Run—or dead.

JOANNA WAYNE

AK-COWBOY

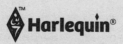

TORONTO NEW YORK LONDON
AMSTERDAM PARIS SYDNEY HAMBURG
STOCKHOLM ATHENS TOKYO MILAN MADRID
PRAGUE WARSAW BUDAPEST AUCKLAND

To my good friends Patsy and Hill. Hill for his law enforcement expertise and willingness to share the information. To Patsy for putting up with me on the golf course when my mind is too convoluted with the current manuscript for me to concentrate on the game.

ISBN-13: 978-0-373-69531-7

AK-COWBOY

Copyright © 2011 by Jo Ann Vest

Recycling programs for this product may not exist in your area.

ABOUT THE AUTHOR

Joanna Wayne was born and raised in Shreveport, Louisiana, and received her undergraduate and graduate degrees from LSU-Shreveport. She moved to New Orleans in 1984, and it was there that she attended her first writing class and joined her first professional writing organization. Her debut novel, *Deep in the Bayou,* was published in 1994.

Now, dozens of published books later, Joanna has made a name for herself as being on the cutting edge of romantic suspense in both series and single-title novels. She has been on the Waldenbooks bestseller list for romance and has won many industry awards. She is also a popular speaker at writing organizations and local community functions and has taught creative writing at the University of New Orleans Metropolitan College.

Joanna currently resides in a small community forty miles north of Houston, Texas, with her husband. Though she still has many family and emotional ties to Louisiana, she loves living in the Lone Star State. You may write Joanna at P.O. Box 852, Montgomery, Texas 77356.

Books by Joanna Wayne

HARLEQUIN INTRIGUE

955—MAVERICK CHRISTMAS
975—24/7
1001—24 KARAT AMMUNITION*
1019—TEXAS GUN SMOKE*
1041—POINT BLANK PROTECTOR*
1065—LOADED*
1096—MIRACLE AT COLTS RUN CROSS*
1123—COWBOY COMMANDO#
1152—COWBOY TO THE CORE#
1167—BRAVO, TANGO, COWBOY#
1195—COWBOY DELIRIUM*#
1228—COWBOY SWAGGER^
1249—GENUINE COWBOY^
1264—AK-COWBOY^

*Four Brothers of Colts Run Cross
#Special Ops Texas
^Sons of Troy Ledger

CAST OF CHARACTERS

Tyler Ledger—The second to youngest son of Troy Ledger—a soldier home on leave.

Julie Gillespie—She's investigating a cold case that someone will kill to keep secret.

Troy Ledger—Tyler's father. Released from prison on a technicality, he is obsessed with finding his wife's killer.

Sean and Eve Ledger—Tyler's brother and sister-in-law.

Dylan and Collette Ledger—Tyler's brother and sister-in-law who have a house on Willow Creek Ranch.

Muriel Frost—Murdered eighteen years ago, but her killer was never arrested.

Sheriff Caleb Grayson—He originally investigated the death of Muriel Frost and he doesn't like his work questioned.

Sheriff Glenn McGuire—Local sheriff and father of Collette.

Zeke Hartwell—Handyman who worked for Muriel Frost.

Guy Cameron—Muriel Frost's former employer.

Candice Cameron—Guy's wife and former friend of Muriel Frost.

Abby—Owns the local diner and knows everything that goes on in Mustang Run.

Chapter One

Julie Gillespie checked her rearview mirror. There was no sign of the black car that she'd feared might be following her when she'd pulled onto this two-lane black-top road a few miles back. The driver of the other car must have turned off on one of the dirt roads. Probably just a rancher rushing home to his cattle.

Paranoia was a bitch.

But New Orleans was behind her now and she was off and running on a new case, icy cold, but one that she was dead set on solving.

This was Julie's first trip back to the Texas Hill Country in many years and she was already enchanted with the scenery. She knew about Lady Bird Johnson's wildflower legacy, but she'd never imagined the roadside blooms would be so abundant.

There was only a scattering of orange, red and yellow in the late March mix. The Indian blankets, goldenrods, buttercups and countless others would come later, but the bluebonnets were profuse.

She rounded a curve and a sea of brilliant blue stretched out as far as she could see. The wind tousled the blossoms so that they looked like gently swaying ocean waves. A few heads of cattle grazed in the distance, adding a Texas perfection to the vista.

Julie lowered her window and breathed in the smell of clean air, flowery perfume and the scent of recent rain. Apparently she'd just missed a downpour that had left the road wet and the ditches filled with water. A bank of low clouds still hovered at the horizon, but there were patches of blue directly overhead.

She turned her attention back to the road as she topped a hill. Good move since an oncoming pickup truck had drifted across the yellow line and was crowding her lane.

She swerved to miss it and skidded onto the shoulder. Adrenaline fired through her as she fought the wheel and tried to pull her white Ford Fusion back onto the blacktop.

To no avail. She careened through a shallow ditch and slammed into a barbwire fence post as the guy who'd unwittingly caused the accident sped out of sight. What a jerk.

The wooden post toppled and the strands of knotted wire drooped almost to the ground. She groaned. Now she'd have fence repairs to pay for out of her meager savings.

Jerking the gear into Reverse, she gunned the engine. The back tires spun like crazy, throwing globs of mud behind her. The car refused to move. Could this get any worse?

She opened the door and stamped her way to the rear of the car for a close-up assessment of her situation as mud smeared her sandals and splattered her bare legs. No visible damage so far to the car, but she was clearly stuck.

She could call a tow truck or wait and see if some passing rancher in a heavy pickup would stop and pull her out of the mire. The second option would be a lot cheaper.

Waiting wouldn't hurt—unless she was being followed. That seemed more unlikely by the minute. Any tail worth his salt would have caught up with her by now.

Still, once she'd checked the front of the car and discovered only a dented bumper, she climbed back inside and locked her doors. And just in case someone who looked suspicious stopped before the helpful rancher she needed, she got her cell phone ready to punch in 9-1-1.

When not one car had passed her in five minutes, Julie climbed out of the car, opened the trunk and retrieved her camera. If she was going to be stranded in what looked like paradise, she might as well capture the beauty.

Too bad she hadn't worn jeans for traveling instead of her best white shorts and a bright blue scoop-necked T-shirt. Careful not to get scratched, she maneuvered her body over the barbwire, landing in the bluebonnet-covered pasture.

Adjusting her lens and aiming her camera, she began snapping photo after photo as she wandered the quiet pasture. Things were going swimmingly—until the horns of a ferocious-looking bull appeared in her viewfinder.

Her pulse skyrocketed. Her hands shook. She left the camera to swing on the cord around her neck as she raced back to the downed fence. She didn't stop for breath until she was safely on the other side. Only there was nothing safe about it.

The bull was still heading in her direction, albeit slowly, and she doubted the downed fence would present any more challenge for him than it had for her. Kicking out of her sandals, she climbed onto the hood of the car and shouted warnings to the bull.

But the bull wasn't coming to the fight alone. He was followed by reinforcements, none of which seemed fazed by her threats of what she'd do if they didn't back off. Forced to pursue drastic measures, she yanked off her belt and started popping it like a whip at the approaching cattle.

She looked around for help. Not even a tractor in sight. She was on her own. And she'd thought looking for a killer might be dangerous.

SMOOTH, BUT DAMP SURFACE. Enough curves to keep it interesting. And no land mines or snipers waiting to sabotage him around the next turn. Roads in the Texas Hill Country were definitely a welcome change from the mountainous, Taliban-infested area of Afghanistan that Tyler Ledger had left three days ago.

That didn't, however, eliminate the chance that he was about to encounter a fiery explosion just miles ahead.

Tyler was on the verge of crashing head-on with his volatile past.

He had been only eight years old when the bottom had fallen out of his innocent world. It had started as a normal school day. It had ended in a tragedy beyond comprehension.

His mother was dead, shot three times and left in a pool of blood on the floor next to the rough stone hearth where he'd placed his boots to dry the night before.

That was just over eighteen years ago. The images from that day were seared into his brain. Beyond that, his boyhood on the ranch was pretty much a blur. Even the memories of his mother were mostly from stories his grandmother had told him before she'd died and from things his brothers had said when they'd gotten together over the years.

He'd been raised by one of his mother's aunts, a stern woman with a brow puckered from a lifetime of scowls. Aunt Sibley had lost her husband and her only daughter in a boating accident years before she took him in and the grief had turned her insides to sour mush.

She did her best with Tyler, though she never let him forget the sacrifice she was making to feed and clothe him. Her main priority seemed to be her constant reminders that if he didn't expect too much from life, he wouldn't be disappointed. The logic of that philosophy had resonated with him even though his aunt's unyielding, humorless ways hadn't.

Which was one reason why he wasn't counting on much to come from this trip to Mustang Run and the Willow Creek Ranch. The other thing his aunt had preached to him was that his father was a heartless beast who'd killed his wife and the mother of his five sons. And this was the father Tyler was on his way to see for the first time since Troy Ledger had been sentenced to life in prison.

Now Troy was out on a technicality and still insisting he was innocent. Maybe he was. Maybe he wasn't. If he was guilty, he could rot in hell for all Tyler cared.

But two of Tyler's brothers were now totally convinced their father was not only innocent, but a man of honor.

Sure he was. So honorable he'd forgotten he had sons until he needed them again.

Tyler wasn't looking for a father eighteen years after the fact, he just wanted to get a handle on where he'd come from. Examine his roots. Walk the ranch where he'd spent the first eight years of his life.

Reconnecting with his brothers Sean and Dylan would be an added bonus, but he wasn't even sure that would turn out well. He had his life figured out. Work hard. Play hard. Fight hard. And don't trust anyone enough to let them get close to you.

Those simple rules had served him well.

Which is why he should have gone to Vegas or to spring break with a bunch of college coeds in wet T-shirts instead of to the Texas Hill Country. He really needed this vacation.

War was hell. He'd been fighting hard. Now he needed to play with that same fervor.

But he was here. He might as well try to enjoy the scenery and the…

Entertainment!

Tyler burst into laughter in spite of his mood and slowed to enjoy the view as he pulled onto the shoulder. He came to a stop a few feet from a ditched car with the hottest, whip-cracking hood ornament he'd ever seen.

Now he was talking vacation.

Chapter Two

Julie watched the black car pull to a stop on the shoulder a few yards behind her. Paranoia surged again. The car could be the same one that she'd thought was following her earlier. Even the front grill looked familiar.

She looked back at the bulls. One was nudging the fence. Two others had stuck their heads over the top of the downed wire to taste some tall weedy stems. Probably building energy for their attack.

The car door opened and a man stepped out and onto a high, dry spot with no mud to smudge his spotless boots. He looked muscled, rock hard—and gorgeous. He also looked too much the cowboy to be one of the New Orleans thugs that she'd feared might still be looking for her.

Julie stared warily as he approached.

The cowboy tipped his hat and grinned, a kind of half smile that would have made her fall into immediate lust under ordinary conditions.

"Most people use the gate," he teased.

"Now why didn't I think of that?" After a quick look

back at the dangerous livestock, she stared him down. "Are you following me?"

"No, but I would have if I'd known it was showtime."

He was clearly fighting to keep from laughing.

"There's nothing funny about my situation. If you were any kind of gentleman at all, you'd be running off the bulls instead of standing there making wisecracks."

"Bulls?"

"Yes, bulls." She pointed at the animals to make her point. "Can't you see those horns?"

His smile took over his face. "They're Texas longhorns. Two of them are steers. One's a heifer. No bulls in sight."

"Bulls, steers, what's the difference?"

"Don't let the steers hear you say that." He walked over and herded the animals away from the fence. Then, picking up the downed post, he righted it and twisted it back into the hole it had been knocked out of. The muscles in his arms flexed impressively as he worked.

"That should keep the wild beasts at bay. Name's Tyler," the cowboy said, extending a hand to help her off the hood of the car.

"I'm Julie," she said, glancing over her shoulder to check out the horned cattle. "How do you know the fence will hold?"

"I figure if it doesn't, I can always get you to crack your whip a few times and protect us."

The blush climbed to her cheek. She ignored his hand and slid off the front fender of the car on her own.

He walked around to study the back wheels and the hole she'd dug herself into while revving the engine.

She joined him, all too aware of the mud that was drying in mottled streaks from her knees to her toes. "I'll need to call a tow truck."

"Why bother? I suspect every rancher around here has a truck heavy enough to pull you from the ditch."

"Does that include you?"

"No. All I have is the rented car you see. I'm on vacation."

"Oh, so you're only a fake cowboy."

"You could say that. Where are you heading?"

"To Willow Creek Ranch."

"Really?"

"Yes. I'm going to see Troy Ledger," she admitted. "Have you ever heard of him?"

"Isn't he the man who went to prison for murdering his wife?"

"That's the one."

"In that case, why don't I give you a lift there and you can get him to pull your car from the ditch?"

"I'm not sure he'll be willing to help me, but I would appreciate the lift."

"Why wouldn't he help you?"

"We've never met, and he didn't invite me."

"Then by all means, I should give you a lift. I wouldn't want to miss the surprise party."

"Okay, but first I need to get my things from the car. I have material in there that I wouldn't want to fall into the wrong hands."

"Sounds intriguing."

"It is, but it's nothing you'll want to get involved in."

"Risky business?" he asked.

"It could turn out to be quite dangerous," she said. That should keep him from making fun of her—and it was also true. "So you'll just want to drop me off at Willow Creek Ranch and be on your way."

"Yes, ma'am," he drawled. "I'll keep that in mind."

TYLER FOLLOWED THE DIRECTIONS Julie gave him for driving to the ranch where he'd been heading all along. He considered telling her his last name, but decided the conversation would likely be far more interesting if she continued to think he was merely a vacationing stranger.

Not to mention that she hadn't offered her last name and was hinting of mysterious secrets.

She was fascinating. The girl-next-door type, if you were lucky enough to have a neighbor with a to-die-for body. He'd never been.

But the body wasn't nearly all she had going for her. There was the cute turned-up nose, full, enticing lips, hay-colored hair pulled into a ponytail that bounced with every move of her head. And not to be shortchanged was the endearing blush when she was the least bit embarrassed and the most expressive blue eyes he'd ever seen.

"How did you choose this part of Texas for a vacation?" she asked.

"I lived here, years ago."

"Where do you live now?" she asked.

"Mostly in Afghanistan for the last four years. I'm in the army."

"From what I hear on the news, it's incredibly dangerous in Afghanistan now."

"It's no picnic in a field of bluebonnets," he teased.

"Ha ha."

"Sorry, but that was some scene back there."

"Get over it. Are you back in the States for good?"

"Afraid not." Tyler decided it was time for a few questions of his own. "Why didn't you let Troy Ledger know you were coming?"

"I was afraid he wouldn't see me since I want to question him about his wife's death."

"Can't say that I'd blame him."

"Yes, but actually, I'm even more interested in the murder of Muriel Frost. She was about the same age as Helene Ledger and murdered in a similar manner in a neighboring county just six months before Helene was killed."

"Do you think Troy Ledger killed both women?"

"It's possible, but judging from the way he's been looking for Helene Ledger's killer, my gut instinct is that he didn't kill either one."

"A jury convicted him," Tyler reminded her, the way his aunt and grandparents had reminded him countless times over the years.

"Innocent men go to jail all the time." She turned to face him, talking as much with her hands as her mouth. "You see the thing is, Troy Ledger was convicted almost entirely on circumstantial evidence. I mean, sure, Helene Ledger was shot with his gun, but anyone could have found the gun in the bedroom and then shot her with it."

"Circumstantial evidence can still be accurate and anyone can claim to be looking for his wife's murderer."

"Yes, but Troy Ledger was a model citizen, at least he had been ever since marrying Helene. Before that, he was a bit of a maverick—drinking, partying and riding the local rodeo circuits. But that's what youth is for."

"Does that mean you've sown a few wild bales of hay?"

Julie struck a defiant pose. "I've been around."

Tyler seriously doubted that. She was much too innocent looking. "Guess that's where you learned the Indiana Jones routine," he teased.

But the mood between them grew more serious as he made the turnoff to the ranch. "Why are you so interested in old murders?" Tyler asked. "You don't look like a detective."

"I'm an investigative reporter."

Tyler let out a low whistle. "No wonder you don't think Troy Ledger will welcome you with open arms."

Tyler stopped at the entrance to the ranch and stared at the weathered, wooden sign above the old iron gate. Willow Creek Ranch.

Haunting memories attacked, bringing things to the forefront of his mind that he hadn't thought of in years. The smell of chicken frying in the skillet atop the gas range. The family gathered at the big dining room table. His mother's voice singing along with the radio.

The tears in his father's eyes when Troy had been

literally ripped from his arms on the night his father had been arrested. And that was pretty much the last time Troy had acted like a dad.

Tyler pushed the troubling images from his mind. Forget the past. In minutes, the present would become an arsenal of weapons all firing in his direction with no visible means of escape.

Tyler was home, yet even the hard, rocky ground of the war zone had never felt so alien.

JULIE CLOSED AND LATCHED the squeaky gate and then hopped back into the front seat beside Tyler. An unexpected rush of uneasiness churned in her stomach as they bumped along the hard dirt road. Either the ranch itself put off eerie vibes, or Julie was not nearly as undaunted by the prospect of coming face-to-face with Troy Ledger as she'd tried to convince herself.

"They say the Ledger ranch house is haunted," she said.

Tyler continued to stare straight ahead without bothering to respond. She started to say more, but his demeanor had changed. His fingers wound tightly around the steering wheel and his neck and facial muscles were taut.

"If you don't like the idea of visiting a convicted killer, you can just drop me off here and you can turn around and leave," she said.

"Too late for that."

His tone was brusque, but he seemed so lost in his own world that she wasn't even sure the words were meant for her. Her feelings of anxiety swelled. Now not only was she on an isolated ranch with a convicted killer but with a stranger who demonstrated drastic mood changes.

He could have post-traumatic stress disorder. She'd heard that was common with military personnel just home from the battlefront.

Julie understood trauma. She'd lived through her share of it. A few short weeks ago, she'd fully expected to be sleeping with the fishes in Lake Pontchartrain. Surviving that had given her the courage to take on her current task.

She spotted the roofline of the Ledger house first, jutting over the tops of the low trees that surrounded it. The full house didn't come into view until they rounded the last curve and pulled up the gravel drive.

The house where Helene Ledger had been murdered in cold blood in the middle of the day. Killed by three shots fired at close range when any one of them could have ended her life. The mother of five young boys, loved by everyone in the community, all but worshipped by her parents.

The hairs on the back of Julie's neck stood on end as they stopped in front of the house. The claims that Helene's ghost still haunted the place drew vivid images in her mind. She could all but see the woman in white standing at the window, waving for help, just as the locals described her.

Julie took a deep breath and opened her door. She was not a believer in ghosts. Even if they existed, she imagined dead people had better things to do than hang around tormenting people they'd probably never liked anyway or grieving those they'd loved and been loved by.

If people had seen anything at all here while Troy was in prison, it was likely shadows from the mulberry tree that grew next to the house or from the nearby cluster of squatty mesquites.

Before she could thank Tyler for the ride, he had opened his own door and was already sliding from beneath the wheel.

"You don't have to stay," she assured him.

"Actually, I do."

"Suit yourself." She walked in front of him, climbed the steps quickly and was about to ring the doorbell when heavy boots clomped through the wet grass to her left.

Troy Ledger rounded the side of the house and stopped a few feet from the freshly painted wooden steps. She knew it was him from photographs she'd seen, one taken as recently as a few months ago.

It had appeared along with pictures of this house in some paranormal magazine called *Beyond the Grave*. Julie had found the article while doing her research on Troy Ledger.

And here he was, a few feet from her. Tall. Thinning brown hair with touches of gray. Gaunt, with a jagged scar that ran down the right side of his face.

She started to speak, but Troy was staring at the cowboy who stood a few feet behind her.

"Tyler." Troy's gruff voice cracked on the name.

"Yeah. It's me."

The tension between the two men left no doubt that they were not strangers.

And once again, she had talked far too much.

Chapter Three

A choking lump in his chest all but cut off Troy's ability to breathe. Tyler was standing a few feet in front of him. Tyler, his daredevil son who had tried Helene's patience with his tough and mischievous ways. Tyler who had followed Troy around like a shadow from the day he took his first steps.

Not one or two awkward steps in the beginning, the way their other sons had learned to walk. No, Tyler had stood and waddled all the way across the kitchen to grab Troy's leg before he stepped out the back door. Troy had swung him into his arms and taken him with him to the barn.

At two, when Tyler should have been content riding his jump horse, he'd begged to ride the biggest horse they had. At four, he'd kept up with his older brothers and mimicked all their antics while swinging from the rope at the swimming hole. At six, he'd broken his arm while trying to rescue a kitten from the top of an oak tree. At eight...

He stopped himself before he dropped into the abyss.

"Good to see you, son."

"I guess I should have called."

"No reason to, except that I might not have been struck speechless."

"So my showing up like this is not an inconvenience?"

"It's…" Troy searched for the right words and settled on the truth. "I've been waiting for this day." He climbed the steps and joined Tyler and his lady friend on the porch, awkward and embarrassed by the onslaught of emotions that were tearing around inside him like crazed cats.

He'd love to hug his son, but the man staring back at him with the piercing brown eyes seemed all but untouchable.

Tyler rocked back on his heels and looked around. "Ranch looked good when I was driving in."

"Dylan gets a lot of credit for that. He's running the ranch with me. Fact is, he did it all for the first few weeks after my heart attack. Sean helped, too, until he moved out."

"I heard Sean bought his own spread," Tyler said.

"Yeah." Troy wondered if Dylan and Sean knew Tyler was planning this visit. If so, they'd kept it quiet.

"Sean started a horse farm over in Bandera."

"How is that working out for him?"

"Good. He's got lots of plans, but he's getting so many calls to work with and train other folks' horses, he hardly has time to work with his own. Did you hear he got married?"

Tyler nodded. "Both him and Dylan."

"Right. You have two new sisters-in-law and a step nephew. Family's growing. Do Sean and Dylan know you're here?"

"No. I thought I'd just surprise all of you."

"You definitely did that."

The silence grew awkward. Troy turned his attention to the woman standing next to Tyler. Nice looking. About Tyler's age, or maybe younger. No wedding band.

"I'm Julie," the woman said.

"And I'm Troy Ledger. Glad to have you."

"I hate to intrude this way."

"You're not intruding at all. Any friend of Tyler's is welcome here anytime."

"Actually, I only met her a few minutes ago," Tyler said. "I just gave her a lift. She's here to see you."

Troy saw the look that passed between Julie and Tyler, but he couldn't read it. Could be attraction. Might just be tension that had to do with why she was here to see him. If so, he probably wasn't going to enjoy the encounter with her. Nonetheless, he wouldn't let her ruin this moment with Tyler for him.

"Why don't we go inside," Troy offered. "It will be easier to talk in there."

He opened the unlocked door and followed them inside. Tyler had changed a lot but somewhere inside, there had to be a trace of the boy Troy remembered. Hopefully they'd reconnect soon and then he'd feel comfortable clapping him on the back or giving him a fatherly punch to the arm or a quick hug.

But not yet. The past separated them as surely as if they'd been carved apart by a hunter's knife.

ONCE TYLER ENTERED THE HOUSE, images seemed to seep from the walls themselves. He and his brothers constructing elaborate Star Wars sets out of Legos that stretched across the entire family room. Watching Scooby-Doo with his brothers while sitting on that same old leather sofa. It was amazing that it had survived when so little from his old life hadn't.

Tyler stopped and stared out the window just behind the pine end table. He'd once hit a baseball through that top right pane. He'd dreaded what would happen when his dad came home. But instead of being punished, Troy had been impressed with the hit that had sent the ball sailing over the hedges and mesquite trees and all the way to the house.

So many good memories overshadowed by the horrifying one. A sick, hollow sensation rolled in the pit of Tyler's stomach as they passed the stone hearth.

His brothers Sean and Dylan had found a way to merge the past with the present and face that reality every day. Tyler was pretty sure that he never could, though he'd been younger than them at the time of his mother's death. Out of the five sons, only Dakota was younger.

Fortunately, Troy led them straight to the kitchen. He got cold beers for himself and Tyler. Julie opted for water.

"So exactly how did you two hook up?" Troy asked.

Julie explained how her car got stuck when she was

forced off the road by a truck that had swerved into her lane. She left out the best part. There was no mention of the whip.

"And the first person to stop was Tyler," Troy said, once she'd finished her animated description. "Strange, fortunate coincidence, considering you were both on your way to Willow Creek Ranch."

"It was, especially when Tyler failed to mention he was your son." She shot Tyler a quick, accusing glance before turning her attention back to his father. "I'm really glad for this chance to talk to you."

"Then we should get down to brass tacks," Troy said. "But I should warn you that if you're a reporter, I'll call you a tow truck and send you on your way."

Undaunted, Julie took a sip of her water, wiped the condensation from her glass with the napkin Troy had provided and smiled as if she were about to hand him a check from Publishers Clearing House.

"I'm an investigative reporter, but you're not the subject of the investigation."

"So why come here to talk to me?"

"Because I know that you've been covering some of the same ground I have."

"How would you know that?"

"Word gets around and you've made no secret of the fact that you're actively searching for your wife's killer."

Troy rubbed his jaw. "Go on."

"I'm investigating the murder of Muriel Frost," Julie explained. "Have you heard of her?"

Troy's brow furrowed. "Yeah. She was murdered six months before Helene. What of it?"

"I'm hoping you'll share what you've learned with me. Frankly, I can use all the help I can get. A case this cold won't be easy to solve."

"You're right about that. The people who want to talk don't know anything. The people with information won't talk."

Tyler studied Troy. His expression gave nothing away, but the deep grooves around his eyes and mouth and the jagged scar did. His years in prison had killed all signs of the young, energetic father who used to outrun, outride and outswim all of them.

"So what got you interested in the Frost murder case, being as it's icy cold."

"It remains unsolved."

"So do lots of more prominent murder cases."

"Actually, you're partly to blame," she admitted. "You made news when you were released on a technicality and again when one of your fellow inmates escaped and went after the former prison psychiatrist you were protecting."

"Eve. She's my daughter-in-law now."

"I know. She married your son Sean."

"You have done your homework. I still think you're going to have your work cut out for you. That's over in Llano county, and Sheriff Caleb Grayson is very protective when it comes to anything that falls under his jurisdiction."

"He's a public servant. And Muriel Frost deserves the same justice everyone else is entitled to."

"And you're out to get it for them? That's a pretty big order."

"I can't get it for everyone, obviously, but I can start with Muriel Frost."

"Sounds admirable, but if you're here because you think I had anything to do with killing my wife or Muriel Frost, you're wasting your time and mine."

The guy was no easy sale, Tyler concluded. Definitely not a pushover for a cute face and hot body. Or maybe he was. She'd admitted to being a reporter and his dad hadn't ushered Julie to the door.

Julie crossed her mud-splattered legs. "Like I said, I'd just like to collaborate a bit. But in all fairness, if I find out you did kill either one of them, I'll come after you with everything I've got."

Troy rubbed his chin and stared into space. About the time Tyler figured the interview was over, Troy began to nod.

"Fair enough," Troy said. "Tyler and I will get your car out of the ditch. Then we'll set a time to meet and share notes. Are you staying here in Mustang Run?"

"If there's a cheap motel."

"Not one I'd recommend," Troy said. "You can stay here a couple nights if you want. There's plenty of room. Nothing fancy."

Julie glanced at Tyler as if expecting him to protest.

"The more the merrier," he said, not completely sure it would work out that way. But at least with Julie around, he wouldn't be forced into nothing but awkward moments between him and a father who'd become a total stranger.

"I'll get your luggage and *confidential* material out of my trunk," Tyler offered.

Julie followed him to the car. When they reached it, she grabbed the heaviest piece of luggage as if asserting her independence. "Why didn't you tell me that you were one of Troy Ledger's sons?"

"You didn't ask."

"Will my staying here bother you?"

"All depends on what you mean by bother."

"Then just tough it out," she stammered, getting his point and turning away as one of those disarming blushes turned her cheeks an enticing red.

She bothered him plenty already, and for more reasons than the obvious. For one, she didn't look or seem like a hardened investigative reporter. Nor did he think she was totally convinced Troy was innocent.

But then, neither was Tyler.

JULIE ACCEPTED TROY'S invitation to stay at the house and unpack while they went for her car. Which meant the inevitable one-on-one father-son encounter could be put off no longer. The awkwardness was not only tangible when Tyler crawled into the front seat of Troy's new double cab white, pickup truck, it was as solid and impenetrable as a cement wall.

The silence hovered until they'd rumbled over the cattle gap and left the ranch.

"We need to let Sean and Dylan know you're here," Troy said. "They'll want to get together right away."

"I'll give them a call once we get Julie's car out of the ditch," Tyler promised.

"Good idea."

They passed a truck pulling a horse trailer. Troy gave a two-fingered wave without lifting his hand from the steering wheel. "That's Everett Wilson. He's one of the unrelenting and unforgiving, crosses the street to keep from speaking to me if our paths are about to intersect in town."

"Yet you waved at him," Tyler noted.

"Only because I know it irritates him."

The perfect opening for the question that preyed on Tyler's mind. "Why did you return to Mustang Run when you were released from prison?"

"It's home. And it seemed the best place for doing what I have to do."

"To prove you're tougher than your critics?"

When Troy didn't respond to the question, Tyler turned and studied his profile. The muscles in Troy's neck were strained, his gaze straight ahead as if he were staring down a tank—or a ghost.

"I came back to find your mother's killer."

The tone was so defiant that the words were guttural. They ground inside Tyler like grit. Did his father really think that uttering those few words would make a difference?

"I didn't kill your mother, Tyler. Whether or not you believe me is up to you. I've made plenty of mistakes in my life, but I won't cower in guilt for something I didn't do."

After a few minutes of silence, Troy visibly relaxed

his grip on the wheel and glanced toward Tyler. "I didn't mean to come at you like that. You have a right to answers."

Tyler nodded. "I obviously hit a sore spot, but I didn't come back to start a fight." At least he didn't think he had.

"What made you decide to visit? Don't get me wrong, I'm thrilled you're here. It's that you don't seem that excited about it."

"Dylan and Sean sounded so optimistic that I guess I had to see where I fit in this new family scheme of things."

"Where you've always fit. You're my son," Troy said. "You're Helene's son. You're a Ledger."

Right, whether he liked it or not.

"I tried to get in touch with all you boys when I was in prison," Troy said. "Your grandparents got a court order forbidding it."

"I know. Dylan told me." And that had been fine with Tyler.

"Can we just drop this for now?" Tyler said, sorry he'd ever brought it up.

"Sometimes it's better to get everything out in the open," Troy said. "Clears the air. Makes it easier to move on."

"Maybe," Tyler muttered. But he wasn't sure he'd ever be ready to move on if that meant just swallowing whatever his dad piled on the plate.

Talk ceased until the ditched car came into view. Troy slowed and swerved into a U-turn after they'd topped the hill and reached a straight stretch of road. He parked on the shoulder and turned on his emergency lights.

Tyler stepped out of the truck and walked straight to Julie's car. His father stopped to study the tire tracks.

"Lucky she slowed before she veered into the ditch. If she'd slammed into that fence post at the same speed she'd left the highway she could have been seriously injured."

"The mud slowed her down," Tyler said, pointing at the grooves her tires had dug into the wet earth.

"Yeah, we had a gully washer about midnight last night. Rain didn't last long, but the thunder rumbled for hours. And then we had a couple of quick showers today."

"Julie hit the post hard enough to knock it over. I righted it, but it probably needs to be reset," Tyler said, remembering the sight that had captured his attention.

Gorgeous, albeit muddy legs. Slim hips. Perky breasts. Dancing ponytail. Whip-cracking action. A surprise tightening in his groin shocked him back to the situation at hand.

"This is Bob Adkins' spread," Troy said. "I'll let him know so that he can check it out. He'll be surprised to hear you're in town. Probably stop by first chance he gets."

"Should I know Bob Adkins?"

"Probably not, but he remembers all you boys. He's a good man. Honest. Hardworking. Church goer. The kind of friend who doesn't tuck tail and run at the first sign of trouble. He's one of the few who stood by me through it all. Him and Able Drake."

Convicted of murdering your wife was a hell of a lot more than a sign of trouble. "Who's Able Drake?"

"A good friend from way back. He had his troubles then, but he turned his life around. And he's stood by me all the way, even spruced up the old ranch house before I got here. Surprised me with this new truck the day I was released."

"Hell of a friend," Tyler agreed. He jumped the ditch to reach the driver-side door of Julie's car. Surprisingly, it was ajar, though he knew it had not only been closed but locked when they drove away.

"Someone's tampered with the car," he said.

"Probably looking for something to steal," Troy said. "Times are changing, even in this part of Texas."

Or else someone had been specifically looking for the material she'd had him load into his rental car. Her first words to him had been to ask why he was following her. He'd taken the question as ludicrous, but for all he knew, some nefarious character had been tailing her.

If so and the bastard had arrived on the scene before Tyler, she'd have had more than harmless cattle to crack her whip at. His apprehension surged when he saw the note attached to the steering wheel. He squinted in the sunlight to make out the words.

In spite of the scribbled print, the message was clear.

Someone wanted Julie out of Mustang Run—or dead.

Chapter Four

Julie's fingers tightened on the edges of the note Tyler had handed her.

Let dead dogs lie, or join them.

She read it for the third time before dropping the note to the table. "It's just a threat," she said, hoping she sounded a lot braver than she felt. "Investigative reporters get them all the time. They don't mean anything."

"I wouldn't be so sure of that," Troy said.

"I say we bag this in plastic and call the sheriff," Tyler said. "We've only touched the top two corners. He may still be able to get a fingerprint off the surface of the paper."

"I'll make a call to the sheriff's office now," Troy offered. "They'll send a deputy out to pick up the note."

"No, please. I'll take care of it," Julie insisted. "It's far more likely this is from someone in Louisiana. The Frost investigation is just in the beginning stages. Few people even know I'm considering taking it on."

"Do you have a specific someone in mind?" Troy asked.

"Melody Jinks. This kind of drama overkill is just

her style. She thinks she ran me out of New Orleans and she wants to make sure I stay out."

"Why would she run you out of New Orleans?" Tyler asked.

The guy was way too inquisitive. Getting mixed up with him was probably going to prove a big mistake.

"Long story, but I'll send the note to a detective I worked with there. He'll check it out. Believe me, it's nothing to worry about. I'm totally through with the Louisiana business."

Tyler's stare grew piercing. "Exactly what did this Louisiana case entail?"

"It's convoluted and X-rated." She waved her hand as if to dismiss the subject.

"My favorite kind," Tyler said. He took her hand and tugged her over to the brown leather sofa.

An unexpected vibration zinged through her like an electric shock, making it all the harder to fake the appearance of nonchalance as he settled in beside her on the sofa. It would be definitely helpful if the guy had a little less sex appeal.

"I helped uncover a sex ring case," she said. She looked around for Troy, but he'd disappeared, leaving her alone with Tyler. "It made all the cable news channels. You must have heard of it."

"News is in short supply in the Afghanistan badlands. So how about you fill me in on the highlights."

"I'm not your responsibility, Tyler. You're back in the States. Women take care of themselves here."

"So I've heard. I'd still like to hear about the case

and Melody Jinks. Or I can just go online and research it myself. But it'd be nice if you saved me the time."

She took a deep breath while she chose her words, making sure to provide only what was a matter of public record.

"Some prominent Louisiana businessmen and influential politicians backed a mafia-run operation in New Orleans that smuggled in underage females from South American countries."

"For prostitution?"

"Right," she said. "I worked with an inside connection to get the goods on the men responsible. With the help of the NOPD, we were able to follow the money trail all the way to the top. Three New Orleans entrepreneurs and two former politicians are in jail awaiting trial."

"So who is this Melody Jinks?"

She hesitated. Melody's crimes were not a matter of public record, at least not yet.

"She's the wife of one of the politicians. She's being investigated now for possibly lying under oath and trying to obscure justice by destroying evidence. And she blames it all on me. But like I said, my part of the investigation is finished. I'm on Muriel Frost like red beans on rice now."

"Then better switch to white gravy on chicken fried steak."

Tyler stretched his long legs in front of him and slid his arm along the back of the couch, grazing her neck with his muscular flesh. She scooted away from him, determined to squelch the effects of his nearness and raw virility.

"So exactly who knows that you're taking on justice for Muriel Frost?"

Julie stood and walked behind the couch, giving herself some distance from Tyler's piercing eyes and seductive touches. "I'm not free to discuss my sources. And now that I think about it, I don't believe my staying here is a good idea."

"You'd let my questions scare you off from the chance to pick Troy Ledger's brain from inside the magic circle? That doesn't sound like a woman who takes death threats in stride."

"It's not just your questions that concern me."

Tyler's brows arched over his dark, hypnotic eyes. "Then what?"

"I'm adding obstacles to your homecoming."

"Let me worry about that."

"There's no need. Just drive me to the nearest motel."

"Yeah, motels are always safe."

A good point. And she wasn't nearly as convinced that the note was from Melody Jinks as she'd insisted. But she wouldn't let fear stop her from doing what she'd come to do. She wouldn't let Tyler Ledger's sex appeal stop her, either.

"Okay, I'll stay," she conceded and then felt foolish. It wasn't as if she was doing the Ledgers a favor.

"So what's next?" Tyler asked.

"The first thing on my agenda is to visit the house where Muriel was killed."

"That was eighteen years ago. You can't just march in someone's house that long after the fact."

"It's a vacant farmhouse. No one will know."

Troy rejoined them and picked up right on cue. "The house is in bad shape," he offered from where he was leaning against the door facing.

"Have you been to the house?" Julie asked.

"Just two weeks ago. It's been taken over by spiders, roaches and local addicts when they need an isolated place to get high. A lot of the windows are broken and some are boarded over. I doubt you'll find any clues hiding in the rotting wood. I didn't."

"Still, I'd like to see it for myself."

Tyler stood and stuffed his hands into the back pocket of his jeans. "I'll go with you."

"Sorry, I fly solo."

"I haven't applied for the job of assistant. This is just a one-time offer. Roaches in Texas are far more frightening than attacking bulls."

He was never going to let her live down the whip cracking. Julie swallowed the rest of her protest. She had no intention of having him trail her every movement, but having someone to stomp roaches would be a definite advantage.

"When can you leave?" she asked.

Tyler turned to his father. "How far is it?"

"It's just over the county line, but still a good hour's drive, maybe longer."

Tyler turned back to Julie. "Then how about first thing in the morning? By the time we could get there tonight, the sun would be going down and you wouldn't be able to see much inside the house."

"Tomorrow morning's fine," she said. "If there's nothing else, I have some notes I need to look over. And you two need some time alone to get reacquainted."

"Right. Make yourself at home," Troy said. "There are soft drinks and beer in the fridge and some homemade cookies that my daughter-in-law Collette made in that boot cookie jar on the counter."

"Thanks."

"And plan to join us for dinner," he said. "I s'pect the whole family will be over, so it will be a madhouse. But the food is guaranteed to be good."

"I'd be delighted."

Troy had that easy way about him that made her feel right at home and made it all but impossible to think of him as a wife-killer.

But the tension between him and Tyler remained as thick as midnight river fog. Apparently, family ties could strangle as well as bind.

At least Tyler *had* some ties to strangle him.

AFTER A HALF HOUR OF TRYING to force conversation, Tyler had escaped the house with the excuse of needing some exercise. Troy had not offered to go on the walk with him. Instead, he'd seemed as relieved by the break as Tyler.

Strange that returning home was far more taxing on Tyler than living in a constant state of danger and battle fatigue. When he was with his squad, he knew what was expected of him and what the enemy was capable of.

Back at Willow Creek Ranch, he was in a no-man's-land where the adversary resided in the hidden crevices of his own mind.

Splinters of caustic images had bombarded him ever since he'd first driven through the clanging metal gate. They'd become as sharp as shrapnel the second Julie had left him and Troy alone.

Memories of his mother's bloodied body were crippling after all these years. But it was more than the haunting visions that dragged him back into his personal hell. The sensations of loneliness and emptiness that had haunted him for most of his childhood had erupted, as well.

With both parents out of his life and separated from his brothers, he'd felt as if he were drifting in an ocean with no haven in sight.

But he'd been a kid then. He didn't need family now. He'd found a way to tough it out and make a life for himself and it wasn't on this ranch or even in Texas.

So why had he come back?

Forcing his mind away from his own dilemma, he concentrated on Julie. She was hot. There was no doubt about that. She seemed intelligent enough—except that she'd jumped on the invitation to stay at Willow Creek Ranch a little too quickly. He could see why she'd want to pick Troy's mind, but staying in the house with a convicted killer was taking job responsibilities a bit too far. So were death threats.

But what really puzzled him was why she'd decided to investigate a Texas crime that was so cold it could chill a desert when she'd just closed the book on a sizzling hot case in Louisiana.

Tyler swatted a huge mosquito that had decided to feed on his neck. A few minutes later, he rounded the horse barn and the ranch house popped back into view. He spotted two unfamiliar pickup trucks parked at the side of the house.

As he got closer, loud talk and laughter and mouthwatering odors wafted through the open kitchen window. No doubt Dylan and Sean had come over to welcome him home, just as Troy had said they would.

Tyler slowed his pace as dread ground in his stomach. Ordinarily he'd be excited about seeing his brothers. But not here, not on this ranch. They'd found a way to fit in and make peace with their father. Tyler felt as if the man were a complete stranger, an imposter playing the role of a man who'd died in his mind years ago.

Turning away from the house, he looked back at the rolling pastureland and the sun setting just behind the tops of a patch of mesquite trees and one lone pine. A horse neighed in the distance. Wildflowers danced in the early evening breeze. The scene was idyllic. In contrast, his insides were a tempestuous storm.

The back door slammed and he looked again at the house to see his brother Dylan heading his way.

"Welcome home, bro," Dylan called.

Home? Not likely. Not in this lifetime. Not for Tyler.

MADHOUSE HAD BEEN AN accurate description for the family get-together. Tyler couldn't help getting a bit caught up in the joviality as introductions bounced around amid hugs and brotherly punches.

There was no getting around the fact that his brothers looked and sounded great. He studied his new sisters-in-law for a second as introductions were made, trying to get who went with whom straight in his mind. It shouldn't be that difficult.

Dylan's wife Collette had flaming red curls that bounced about her shoulders. The green silky blouse she wore over her form-fitting jeans set off her flashing emerald eyes. Her enthusiasm bubbled like chilled champagne, and he liked her instantly.

Sean's wife Eve was just as stunning, but more reserved and he had the feeling she was sizing him up the same as he was her. She was probably a damn good shrink, though Troy had mentioned this afternoon that she hadn't worked as a psychiatrist since her son's father was murdered.

"This is our son, Joey," Sean said, touching the shoulder of a tow-headed tyke who studied Tyler warily.

Tyler bent to shake his hand. "Hello, there, cowboy. Nice boots you've got on."

Joey stuck one foot in front of him so Tyler could get a better look. "You can get 'em as muddy as you want."

"They look clean and spiffy now," Tyler assured him.

"What's spiffy?"

Sean patted his stepson on the head. "Means they're looking good."

"I'll be six years old next month," Joey said. "I might get a pony."

"Wow. Now that's exciting."

"Yeah." Joey beamed. "I already have a dog. I named him Sparky."

"Nice name."

Joey took hold of Sean's hand. "Sean and Grandpa got him for me."

Grandpa. The word bucked around in Tyler's head like hooves to the temples. He wasn't sure Troy had the right to the title.

"Never saw myself as a dad," Sean said when Joey walked away.

"The kid adores you," Tyler said. "So you must be doing something right."

"I can't imagine a life without Eve and Joey in it."

"I can tell."

According to an email he'd gotten from Dylan, Sean had gone from renegade horse whisperer who disdained romantic relationships to husband and father in record time. But then Dylan had fallen just as quickly for Collette.

It was almost as if Willow Creek Ranch had put a spell—or a curse—on them. Luckily, Tyler wouldn't be here long enough for that to happen to him.

Still, he impulsively looked around for Julie. She was nowhere in sight, though he doubted she could concentrate on work with this much noise to disrupt her.

"Dad said you went out to get your bearings," Dylan said, handing Tyler a cold beer. "Did you get to see much of the ranch?"

"Just what I could get to by foot, but what I saw was impressive."

"We're building the herd slowly, taking our time with choosing good breeding stock."

Tyler took a long swig of the beer. "Makes sense. I did stop at the horse barn. You've got some great-looking mounts."

"Acquiring horseflesh is Collette's department," Dylan said. "She's as good at that as she is at photography."

"Most of my newly acquired knowledge is compliments of Sean," Collette added, "but I do love working with the horses."

"And the lady makes a mean blackberry cobbler," Troy said. He opened the oven. "Catch a whiff of that."

Tyler sniffed as instructed. "Now you're talking my language."

Sean leaned against the kitchen counter. "Guess you don't get a lot of cobbler in Afghanistan."

"Don't recall it ever showing up in my MRE packs."

"Guess you didn't get any good Texas beef, either. I've brought over some steaks," Sean said. "We'll throw them on the grill in a bit while Eve slings together her infamous spring greens and strawberry salad, both fresh from the local farmer's market. Nothing like a real Texas meal to make a man glad he's back in the Lone Star State."

"Me and Grandpa don't do cooking," Joey said. "We're just the eaters."

"I hope I get picked for your team," Tyler said.

Tyler made the effort, but still the family trappings were starting to close in on him like smoke from an enemy explosion. It was as if everyone had put the years of separation and heartbreak behind them.

Almost as if the murder had never happened right here in this house.

"I'll go to my truck and get the cooler with the meat," Sean said.

"I'll help." Tyler gulped down the remainder of his beer and set the glass on the counter with so much force that the clunk seemed to echo around the crowded kitchen. Family skeletons began rattling in his head like a pair of maracas.

Julie stepped though the kitchen door before he could escape out the back. Everyone except Troy turned to stare at her and the room grew completely quiet.

"I hope I'm not interrupting," she said.

Troy stepped beside her. "Not at all. Everyone, meet my houseguest, Julie Gillespie."

The mud was gone from her legs and she'd changed out of the revealing white shorts. But the black skirt and soft pink blouse she was wearing did just as much to fire Tyler's imagination and libido.

It wasn't so much *what* she wore as the way she wore it, oozing femininity and confidence and still looking like a woman you could have a beer with.

Collette was the first to stick out a hand. "It's so nice to meet you."

Dylan grinned. "You've been holding out on us, Tyler."

"She's not with me." The words flew from his mouth a bit more brusquely than he'd intended.

"I'm here to see Troy," Julie said, setting the record straight.

Troy nodded. "She's here to compare notes with me on an old murder."

"So you're a reporter?" Collette asked.

"Yes. An investigative reporter."

The cordiality took an icy plunge.

"Whose murder?" Dylan asked.

"Muriel Frost," Troy answered.

Julie stepped farther into the room and placed her hands on the back of a tall kitchen chair. "Muriel was murdered about the time your mother was and in similar fashion."

"So immediately you thought of Troy Ledger," Sean accused.

Irritation surfaced with surprising force. Tyler could understand where his brothers were coming from, but Julie hadn't exactly forced her way into the house. He was about to defend her, but Troy beat him to it.

"I invited Julie to stay here. If any of you have a problem with that, take it up with me—privately."

The authority in Troy's voice left no doubt who was head of the house.

Eve finally broke the awkward silence that followed. "Excuse the chaos, Julie, but today is a very special occasion and emotions are running high. Troy's son Tyler arrived just this afternoon, as well. He's a soldier, on leave from active duty in Afghanistan."

"Yes, Tyler and I have met. But just so we're all on the

same page here, I'm not here to investigate Troy Ledger, but to coordinate our findings. From what I can tell, he's investigated the Frost murder more extensively than the sheriff's department did at the time of the murder or since."

Her direct and easy manner further diffused but didn't completely eliminate the tension. Talk began to flow again in normal tones. A dog barked at the back door and Joey asked permission to go out and play. Dylan poured Julie a glass of white wine. Eve asked if Julie had been to the Hill Country before.

Only Collette still appeared anxious. She stood in the rear corner of the kitchen with her arms folded over her chest and her lips pulled tight. Clearly her fears about Julie had not been relieved.

"Let's get that cooler," Sean said.

Tyler followed him outside, thankful for the escape.

"Julie seems nice enough," Sean said, "but I'm not easy having a reporter around. Dad's got a right to privacy."

"I didn't invite her to stay," Tyler said. "He did."

"I'm not blaming you. I'm just saying something tells me that she's walking, breathing trouble."

Tyler would have argued the point except that all his battle intuition told him that Sean was right.

IN SPITE OF THE SHAKY beginning, the meal went well, at least for Julie. If she'd had a family, she'd have wanted them to be just like this. Kicking in with the cooking chores. All talking at once. Comfortable with each other. Making her feel welcome though she knew she wasn't.

She represented the past they were trying to escape. Troy Ledger's imprisonment. Helene Ledger's murder.

Tyler wiped a streak of berry juice from his lips. "I haven't had a meal like that in years."

"There's plenty more cobbler," Collette offered.

"One more bite, and I'd explode."

"Anyone else?"

Sean leaned back in his chair and patted his stomach. "Couldn't hold it."

"Not tonight," Dylan said. "Might hit it again for breakfast."

"Yeah, for breakfast," Joey echoed. He licked his lips. "With ice cream."

"Cobbler is not a breakfast food," Eve said, but her smile and fake shock hinted she might give in.

"You ladies relax on the porch, and the men will take care of cleanup," Dylan said.

"Not a chance." Eve jumped up and started gathering the bowls and eating utensils. "It's Tyler's first night on the ranch. You guys need to do your brotherly bonding bit."

Collette picked up the red stoneware baker that held the remainder of the cobbler. "Have you noticed how much more willing Dylan is to take on KP duty now that you have the new dishwasher?"

"Yep." Troy pushed back from the table. "I like it myself. Worth every overpriced cent."

The men helped clear the table before heading out the back door.

Joey watched them leave but didn't ask to join them. "May I watch TV?"

"Did you feed Sparky?" Eve asked.

He grinned as if he knew that question was coming. "I tried to but he didn't come when I called him."

"Then call again."

Joey did—loudly. In minutes, a gorgeous, panting retriever appeared at the back door. Eve let him in and the golden-haired pup rushed over to Joey, jumping on him and licking him as if they'd been separated for months.

"Be sure he has fresh water, too," Eve reminded.

"Yeah, 'cause I bet he's been out chasing squirrels," Joey said, beaming as if that were a laudable accomplishment for a dog. "He loves coming to Grandpa's house."

Julie grabbed a wet cloth and began wiping the counter and the range top, choosing to listen more than talk as the conversation moved to the house that Eve and Sean were refinishing.

"I found the perfect antique handles for the kitchen cabinets at a garage sale in Marble Falls last week," Eve said. "And Sean was able to rescue enough beams from the Fielders' old barn to reinforce the family room ceiling."

"I can't wait to see the finished product."

"That may take awhile. Sean got a call from Carl Upton of Upton Farms in Tennessee. He's having problems with a very expensive racehorse and he wants Sean to take a look at it."

"So Sean is still taking a few horse whisperer jobs,"

Collette said. "I wondered if he'd give that up entirely now that he's starting his own horse farm."

"I don't think he can," Eve answered. "It's in his blood. And he has such a talent for it that I'd never encourage him to quit."

"I don't blame you."

"But right now he's thrilled to have Tyler here," Eve said. "It was so sad how they were all separated after Helene's death and farmed out to various and assorted members of her family."

"Who all believed that Troy had killed their mother," Collette added. "It's amazing any of the boys have given him a chance."

"And now three have come home," Eve said. She handed a bowl she'd just emptied to Collette who was loading the dishwasher. "How's your photography going?"

"Great. I'm primarily focusing on my creative work now and taking care of the horses. But I've agreed to work the Bluebonnet Festival Dance on Thursday night at Memorial Park."

"That should be fun. Maybe I can talk Sean into coming if he's in town." Eve turned to Julie. "You should come, too. And talk Tyler into it. He could use a little Texas two-steppin' after all that time in the Middle East."

Dancing with Tyler. Swaying to the music. His body pressed against hers. The last thing she needed, she warned herself. The hot tingles dancing along her spine paid no attention to her declaration.

"I'm not sure what I'll be doing on Thursday and I definitely can't speak for Tyler," Julie said.

"But if you're still in town and not busy, you should come with or without him," Eve insisted.

"It does sound tempting, but I don't have the right clothes with me for a dance," she said truthfully.

"You could wear what you have on. It's casual and I heard that they're bringing in a great Western band from Austin."

Collette wiped her hands on a kitchen towel and stepped away from the sink though it still held dishes waiting to be loaded into the dishwasher. "Julie's not here for festivals, Eve. She's here to conduct an investigation."

Julie took a deep breath. The gloves had just come off. She worked to keep her tone cordial. "I have no intention of causing trouble for Troy Ledger, but if my being here bothers you, I can stay at a motel in town."

"I'm sure Collette didn't mean it that way," Eve said.

"I don't care where you stay," Collette agreed, "but I don't want Helene's murder and Troy's trial forced onto center stage again. It makes it almost impossible for Troy to move on."

"It's not knowing who killed his wife that keeps him from moving on," Julie argued.

"Julie's right," Eve said. "Troy's obsessed with finding Helene's killer. He was while he was in prison, but he's even more determined now. So if Julie can help him find that peace, then I think we should support her efforts."

Collette took a deep breath and exhaled slowly. Her expression was still grim, but she nodded as if acquiescing. "Just don't go placing blame on Troy. He's innocent, and he's a good man who deserves better."

"Like I said," Julie reiterated, "I'm investigating the murder of Muriel Frost. There's no evidence that suggests that your father-in-law even knew her."

"Evidence and truth are not always the same thing," Collette said. "But if you're determined to go through with your investigation, my father may be able to help you. He's Glenn McGuire, our local sheriff. If you contact him, tell him that you're a friend of mine but it's probably better not to mention Troy Ledger. There's a bit of bad blood between them."

"I appreciate that."

Eve stopped loading dishes and turned to face Julie. "If you're going to stay on here, I should warn you to be careful. This house has strange and formidable powers."

"I've heard stories about the house being haunted," Julie admitted. "I'm afraid I'm a cynic where ghosts are concerned."

"It's not the ghosts you should fear."

"Then what is it?"

"The Ledger charm. Collette and I are living proof of its power to seduce."

"I'll watch for Cupid at every step," Julie promised, thankful for the reduction in tension.

They needn't worry about her and Tyler. The attraction was devastating, at least on her part. But once Tyler found out that she was lying with practically every breath, he'd dump her faster than yesterday's coffee grinds.

It couldn't be helped.

When an hour had passed without the men returning, Collette, Eve, Joey and Sparky decided to take advantage of the evening breeze on the wide front porch. Julie claimed fatigue and retired to the sanctuary of the guest room.

Her footfalls echoed along the length of the narrow hallway. Streaks of moonlight filtered through the bedroom windows and cast a shadowed glow over the paste-colored walls. In spite of her proclaimed cynicism, Julie's mind wandered to the ghost tales that had circulated prolifically right after Troy Ledger's release from prison.

It was easy in the eerie semidarkness to imagine Helene's ghost roaming the halls of the sprawling ranch house. If she was here, then perhaps she'd help Julie find Muriel Frost's killer, especially if that person had also taken Helene's life.

But then if she were going to do that, she would have surely helped her husband already.

Unless Troy really had killed her.

Julie flicked on the guest room light, took a sheaf of notes from the suitcase she'd left open on the bed and dropped into the wooden rocker that overlooked the garden. Flicking through the pages, she located the one listing the similarities and differences in the two murders.

Both Helene and Muriel had been young mothers living in semi-isolated areas. Helene lived in this ranch house. Muriel lived in a rented farmhouse at the end of a quiet blacktop road.

Helene's five sons had been in school that day. Muriel's seven-year-old niece who lived with her had been home ill. She'd witnessed the murder while shuddering in fear behind a staircase.

Helene's clothes had been ripped from her body before she'd been shot three times. Muriel was also found naked and brutally beaten, being shot twice in the head at close range. Nothing had been stolen in either instance. Neither woman had been raped.

Julie's cell phone rang. She grabbed it and answered without glancing at the caller ID.

"Hello."

"Is this Julie Gillespie?"

The voice was male and unfamiliar. Her pulse rose. "Yes. Who is this?"

"Sheriff Caleb Grayson from Llano county. I thought we had an understanding that you were to take your nosy reporting somewhere else."

"As I remember it, you did all the talking. I didn't promise anything."

"Just stay out of my space and you and I will do just fine."

"How far does your space extend?"

"Over every square inch of my county."

"I'm not in your county."

"No, you're over in Mustang Run, and let's keep it that way."

"How do you know where I am?"

"I have my ways. And you're making a big mistake

hanging out with Troy Ledger. He's a killer who'd still be behind bars if some fool judge hadn't figured that black robe gave him precedence over the whole damn jury that convicted him."

"Why do you care what I do, Sheriff? Why does my investigating a cold case from your files bug you so much?"

"I just don't like some pseudo journalist like you trying to make my deputies look like a bunch of country bumpkins with no clue how to conduct an investigation. If the evidence had been there, we'd have found Muriel Frost's killer. End of story."

"Is that all?"

"Get in your car and keep moving, Julie. We don't need your kind around here."

"Leave while I'm still breathing?"

"Leave before you start more trouble than you can handle."

The connection clicked and went dead.

Julie gritted her teeth and went back to her notes. She would not be frightened off by an arrogant, obstinate sheriff. There was far too much riding on this case.

LET DEAD DOGS LIE, *or join them*.

The words printed on the note had been troubling Tyler all evening though neither he nor Troy had mentioned the threat to Dylan and Sean. Having a reporter in the house seemed to upset them enough.

In contrast, they'd eagerly welcomed Tyler. He liked seeing his brothers and he'd definitely needed a break from the pressures of battle. But the stress of trying to fit into this new family scheme of things was like being forced to coat your ice cream with vinegar.

He couldn't swallow it. Innocent or guilty, Troy Ledger was still the stranger he'd become when Tyler had needed a father most.

But Julie intrigued him. The first sight of her cracking that whip would fuel a thousand fantasies. Maybe he'd be lucky and she'd visit his dreams tonight.

Ten minutes before the bewitching hour, yet the house was totally quiet. He was caught somewhere between the radical time changes distance imposed. For all his body knew, it was the middle of a sunless day.

Searching the cabinets, he located several bottles of liquor, most of them full. He chose the whiskey and poured a couple fingers' worth of the amber liquid into a short glass and walked into the family room.

The room where his mother's body had been found. He stared at the stone hearth and images that floated deep in the fog of childhood memories exploded in his mind in vibrant color. Her body covered in a bleached white sheet. Her dark hair matted in a sticky crimson mass. His mother's beautiful eyes, yet when he'd looked into them that day, she hadn't been in there. It was that blank stare of death that had frightened him most.

Taking a sip of the whiskey, he savored the slow burn as the liquid traveled down his throat. Then he forced his eyes from the hearth to a small desk against the back wall of the room. A laptop computer beckoned. Tyler crossed the room, switched it on, and clicked on the internet icon.

Sliding into the uncomfortable wooden desk chair,

he slid the cursor to Google and typed in *New Orleans sex ring*. In seconds, dozens of sites were displayed. He selected the most promising and took another sip of the drink as the article loaded.

"Prominent New Orleans Businessmen and Two State Senators Arrested in Underage Sex Scandal," the title read.

He scanned the article, digesting the brunt of the information. The details were all there, as sordid and depraved as you'd find in the latest thriller. There was no mention of Julie Gillespie.

He read three more articles with the same results. No Julie.

Disgruntled to the point of marching into her bedroom and demanding to know why she'd lied, he searched Google for her name. He found a few articles written by a woman named Julie Gillespie for the *Times-Picayune* in New Orleans, fluff pieces to appeal to locals. Not one investigative piece of work bore her byline.

When he was about to give up, she showed up again, this time under the moniker of Julie G. The accompanying photo left no doubt that teenage advice columnist Julie G and the woman sleeping down the hall were one and the same.

Tyler clicked again and an enlarged picture and a sample from her column claimed the entire screen.

Dear Julie
I really like this boy in my second period study hall, but when I try to start a conversation with

him, he ignores me. How can I tell if he's shy or just not interested?

Investigative reporter? Like hell she was.

And he seriously doubted that one of her lovesick teens was responsible for the note found on her car today.

But someone had threatened her. Julie was in danger. The burning question was: Why?

And if she wasn't an investigative reporter, what was she really doing in Texas and why had she come to see Troy Ledger?

Possibilities stormed his mind. Things like her selling the story of Troy Ledger's life in the haunted house where he'd murdered his wife to some cheap gossip magazine.

It wasn't the first time trusting a woman had backfired on Tyler. Hopefully one day he'd learn his lesson.

Tyler carried his glass back to the kitchen and started down the hall to the guest bedroom. He slowed at the sound of footsteps and movement at the end of the hall. Julie, as if she knew he was coming to confront her and saving him the trouble. He stopped and waited for her to reach him.

"I was just going for a glass of water," she whispered. "I didn't realize anyone was still up."

She crossed her arms tightly over her chest as if afraid that even in the dark, he'd glimpse the outline of her nipples beneath her pajamas. She pulled herself in to squeeze past him.

He put up an arm and blocked her escape. Leaning toward her, he placed his mouth to her ear.

"Dear Julie. This woman I met today fed me a line of bull a mile long. I don't like being lied to. I'm thinking she'd better start leveling with me—now!"

Chapter Five

Julie took two steps backward since there was no going forward with Tyler blocking her path. "Keep your voice down," she whispered through clenched teeth. "You'll wake Troy."

"Maybe we should. I think he'd be interested in learning that you're no more an investigative reporter than I'm Lady GaGa."

"You wasted no time in checking me out."

"I'm not the most trusting of guys."

"Obviously. It's late, Tyler. Can we have this conversation in the morning?"

"It's morning in several time zones right now. Take your pick."

He stepped closer and to her dismay, a shudder of awareness ripped though her.

"Fine," she muttered, giving in. "But I'd rather not talk in the hallway."

"I'm easy. My room or yours?"

"Mine," she said, defiantly. At least in hers she had material to back up her story—and a robe to pull over her thin pajamas. Not to mention enough space to move so far away from Tyler that she wouldn't catch the musky, masculine scent of him with every breath.

She turned and marched to her room without her water. When she didn't hear Tyler following her, she picked up her pace. She could just go into the room and lock the door behind her, but something told her that wouldn't work with Tyler. He'd make a ruckus until she unlocked it—or knock the door down. With his muscles, he easily could.

By the time he actually stepped inside her room, she'd shrugged into a short blue terry robe, switched on both the desk lamp and the one next to the bed. Then she pushed back the thick privacy curtain and opened the sliding door that led to the courtyard garden.

She fanned the notes she'd been studying earlier across the desk. She'd give Tyler as much as she had to get him off her case. Nothing more.

"You forgot this," he said, holding out a large glass of ice water.

Darn it! Leave it to Tyler to do something thoughtful just when she was working up a good burst of antagonism toward him.

He closed the door behind him. She walked over and stood by the desk, trying desperately to find a way to put him on the defensive. "I wrote an advice column for teenagers," she said. "That isn't against the law, so what's your problem?"

"I could care less what you wrote. You lied about being an investigative reporter when you moved in here today. What else have you lied about? What is it you want from Troy?"

"Information about Muriel Frost, just as I said."

She picked up her list of similarities and differences and handed it to him. "True enough that I haven't had extensive experience as an investigative reporter, but everybody has to start somewhere. And I proved in New Orleans that I'm up to the task."

Julie drank half the glass of water. She really had been thirsty.

Tyler gave the list a quick once-over and dropped it back to the desk. "Looks impressive, but I've spent the last hour reviewing information on the New Orleans case. Numerous investigators were identified. Your name never came up."

Julie's hands flew to her hips. The dratted robe gaped open, making her blush and totally destroying the effect of warranted anger she'd been shooting for.

She pulled the robe tight again and dropped to the edge of the bed. "The police and reporters weren't big on sharing accolades, especially with me."

"How did writing fluff articles and advice pull you into such a disgusting mess?"

"I received a Dear Julie letter from a young woman who claimed she'd been kidnapped in Guatemala, smuggled into the U.S. and was being held captive and forced to work as a prostitute."

Tyler gripped one of the bedposts and stared down at her. His gaze was intense, his expression wary. "How did you handle that?"

"At first I suspected it might be a ruse. I get lots of those. Kids with too much time on their hands made up bizarre problems and sent them to me for kicks, hoping I'd answer them in the newspaper."

"How did you decide this was on the up-and-up?"

"It was written in broken English and half the words were misspelled. I took a chance it might be legitimate, so I brought it to the police who promptly ignored it.

"I later realized that was because a huge number of them were taking bribes from the trash who were running the operation. So I had no choice but to take matters in my own hands."

"Meaning?"

"I disguised myself as a man."

"I can't imagine you fooled anyone."

"When I decide to do something, I do it well," she assured him.

"Touché. Go on."

"I went down to the French Quarter in search of very young prostitutes. It took only a few inquiries before someone recommended I contact a man they called Cruz. They even described him and told me the bar where I could find him."

"That was quite a risk on your part."

She shook her head. "That was the easy part. The hard part was finding a cop who'd take me seriously. I finally found a bulldog of a detective who wasn't on the take. Between the two of us, we collected enough evidence to get the media interested. After that the NOPD had to investigate. The rest is history."

"I don't see how it can be considered history if you're still getting death threats."

"I may have been wrong about the threat being

from Melody. There's been a new development," she admitted.

"Since this afternoon?"

"Since dinner."

Though she hadn't planned to, she told Tyler about the call from Sheriff Grayson. "I think he may have put that note on my car to scare me off the Frost case."

"What makes you think that?"

"He practically threatened me on the phone, indicated I'd be in real trouble if I didn't move on."

"So are you giving up and moving on?"

"Hardly. I refuse to be bluffed by some arrogant sheriff who thinks he owns an entire Texas county."

"I guess that means our little road trip is still on."

"It's definitely on for me."

"In that case, I'll see you in the morning."

His reaction caught her completely off guard. She'd expected him to kick her out of the house or at least tell her that she was crazy. Every time she was all set to dislike him, he threw her a curve.

She didn't want to like him. She didn't want to feel anything at all for him.

Still, she followed him to the door and leaned against it. "Does that mean you believe me?"

"It means I don't like arrogant sheriffs. Now get some sleep." He touched a finger to her chin and trailed it along her neck to her collarbone. "And get a tie for your robe. I haven't seen female breasts up close and personal in a long, long time, and I'm not known for my restraint."

She looked down as he walked away. The robe was

open again and her pebbled nipples were pushing like bullets against the silky fabric of her pajamas.

This time she wasn't sorry. Tyler Ledger might not fully believe her—smart man. But at least she wasn't the only one who could ignite a bit of sexual interest.

TYLER SHOVED A GAUZY CURTAIN of cobwebs aside. A hairy spider fell to the floor and scurried across the thick carpet of dust that covered the old plank floorboards. A large field rat raced it to a sizable crack that looked as if it had been gnawed into the back corner of the room.

"Nice setting for a horror movie."

"It was," Julie said. "Only it was enacted years ago."

Tyler stepped over a worn blanket, and a pile of garbage that consisted mostly of chicken bones and empty fast-food bags. Two huge roaches ducked under the blanket.

"Do you have any idea how long it's been since anyone's lived here?" he asked.

"Around seventeen years, if the information Kara Saunders gave me was correct."

"Who's Kara?"

"She was a friend and coworker of Muriel."

"Does she live around here?"

"Not any more. She remarried and moved to Lafayette, Louisiana about ten years ago, which made it a lot more difficult to track her down."

"But not difficult enough to keep you from finding her."

"Right. I stopped by to see her on my way to Texas."

"How does she feel about your investigating the case?"

"She thinks I'm wasting my time and she told me flat out that she doesn't want the case legally reopened. Of course that was after I persuaded her to talk to me at all. She refused to even see me at first."

"But then she figured the only way she could get rid of you was to answer your questions."

"Something like that."

Tyler sympathized with Kara Saunders. He figured standing in Julie's way once she set her mind to it would be like trying to stop a tank with a .22.

"Kara said that as far as she knew, the house was only rented once after the murder. Fully furnished since no one claimed Muriel's belongings. And the couple who rented it stayed less than a month."

"Why was that?"

"Superstition. They claimed they heard screams in the night and that doors slammed and things went missing from their closets and cupboards. Word got around after that, and apparently no one would rent or buy the house."

"Uninvited guests can be a pain. I'm not talking about you," he added quickly before she misread him, got peeved and decided again to take her room-and-board business elsewhere.

His reasons for wanting her to stay on at the ranch weren't completely clear in his own mind, nor were they particularly noble. For one thing, she gave him an excuse not to spend his every waking hour with Troy.

Mostly it had to do with the way Julie got his motor

running with just a sway of her shapely hips or a glimpse of those dynamite legs.

But the attraction wasn't all sexual. Her determination fascinated him. Back her into a corner and she threw those hands to her hips and stood her ground. And, he loved the flash of fire in her eyes when she talked of solving this case.

None of which meant she had much chance of succeeding.

Julie jumped out of the way of an escaping daddy longlegs spider.

"It's harmless," Tyler said. He did, however, swat at a giant mosquito that was sucking blood from his forearm.

Julie kicked a mustard-smeared hamburger wrapper out of her way. "I'm guessing the food scraps were donated by the druggies Troy mentioned."

"Doing their part for the survival of the roach and rodent species," Tyler said. He followed her to the one piece of furniture in the room, a hardwood bookshelf that held a few moldy books, some tattered newspapers and yellowed magazines. The newspapers were covered in rat excrement.

To Tyler's surprise, Julie pulled a pair of thin rubber gloves from the pocket of her blue shorts.

"You came prepared," he said.

"Your father gave me the gloves while you were showering this morning," she said, tugging them on. She reached into her pocket for a second pair. "He sent these for you. And there's a thermos of coffee in the car, as well, also thanks to your father."

Who'd have expected that? Tyler took the gloves, but stuffed them in the back pocket of his jeans. "I don't see how you'll get any evidence from this house that's not totally contaminated."

"I'm not sure I will," she agreed. "But visiting the crime scene seems the logical place to start an investigation." She picked up a newspaper, shook it gingerly to remove a few layers of grime and then looked until she found a page that still had the date intact.

"It's from a few days before the murder," she said. Her voice took on a husky tremor, and she coughed to clear the stale, mold-filled air from her throat.

He reached up and knocked away an unidentifiable bug crawling up the back of her neck. "Are you sure all good investigative reporters started like this?"

"Yes, but this is your vacation. You don't have to stay, Tyler. I'm perfectly capable of handling this on my own."

"And miss all the fun? Besides, I'm used to scorpions, spiders, poisonous snakes and insects previously unknown to civilized man."

He followed her to what once was the kitchen. Faded stains that might or might not be blood painted eerie shapes on the floor and splattered bizarre designs on the peeling wallpaper behind a scarred oak table.

"Is this the room where the murder took place?" he asked, sure Julie would know.

"She was shot in the entranceway, just below the staircase. But according to old newspaper reports, deputies at the time surmised the attack started in here. Kara said Muriel was frying chicken when the man broke into her house, though I'm not certain how she knows that."

"It's a small town. I'm sure a lot of true and false information about the investigation circulated."

"I guess. Kara said the man took her by surprise and that she never had a chance. And according to every report I read, the battery was extremely brutal."

In spite of her earlier bravado, Julie's face went pale as she stared at the stains. If she stayed in this business, she'd toughen up, become desensitized to this kind of gore, but Tyler could tell she wasn't there yet.

Julie swayed, and he moved quickly, wrapping his arms around her waist to steady her. A rush of unexpected heat and stirring shot through him.

"Sorry," she said. "Guess I'm not the pro I'd like to be."

"You'll get there." He stepped away. He was only in Mustang Run for a few days, he reminded himself. Enjoying Julie's company was one thing, but falling for a woman he had no reason to trust was just plain crazy.

He tagged along as Julie trudged from room to room, examining the few remaining pieces of furniture. An antique desk and what appeared to be slats from a bed in one room. An old coatrack in another. An open cedar chest pushed against the wall in a closet beneath the staircase.

Julie stopped and examined each piece of furniture, stroking the desk almost lovingly as if she expected coaxing would seduce it into giving up some long-kept secret.

She checked every drawer and then had Tyler go back to his car for a flashlight and a canvas tote full of plastic zip bags she'd brought with her but had forgotten to bring in.

Once retrieved, she directed the beam into the dark corners of the chest. A giant scorpion crawled up the side and had almost reached her fingertips before either of them saw it. She jumped back and fell against him.

"We've got to stop meeting like this," he said, managing a humor that didn't compute with his raging testosterone.

They left the empty chest and moved on to search every nook and cranny of the gossamer-veiled house, even the backs of closet floors and the hard-to-reach spots at the top of closet shelves.

When they finished with the first floor, they went to the second, a huge, open area with beams but no dividing walls. There were built-in shelves beneath a row of high windows, empty except for a half-missing set of ancient encyclopedias. Two old rockers, a battered workbench and a rolltop desk with missing drawers and doors hanging askew from broken hinges had been pushed against a back wall.

Tyler stopped at the foot of the stairs to the attic while Julie performed a fruitless search-and-rescue mission of the desk. "Do you think the furniture in the house now belonged to Muriel Frost?" he asked

"I'm guessing that it did, probably what was left of her furnishings after vandals took what they wanted."

"You're probably right," Tyler agreed. "Do you know who owns the house?"

"Guy and Candice Cameron. They were also Muriel's employer at the time she was murdered. Kara said they let her live here rent free while she worked for them."

"Nice benefit plan. Of course, I've got the same thing with the army. What kind of business are the Camerons in?"

"They were in real estate when Muriel worked for them. Now they're successful land developers."

"Nice for them. How successful?"

"Billionaire range. They've built several upscale golf course neighborhoods, a resort and shopping center near Marble Falls. And that's just what I know about."

"I'm surprised they've held onto this old house for so long."

"They also own the acreage surrounding it which they lease to a neighboring rancher. That information I got from public legal records."

Julie had done her field prep. He'd give her that. She roamed the area for another thirty minutes, basically accomplishing nothing.

"A beautiful day is a terrible thing to waste," Tyler said. "Are you ready to go?"

She shook her head, sending her ponytail into a bouncy dance. "Not even close. I want to check the attic and then walk around outside."

"Do you have any idea what you're looking for?"

"No, but I'll know if I find it."

Tyler grimaced, but took advantage of Julie's rear view as he followed her and her swaying hips up the steep attic steps.

Unfortunately, the attic proved as depressing as the

rest of the house. The window facings had rotted and years of wind and rain had deteriorated the walls and floorboards until some areas had collapsed.

But not the area along the window wall where a large metal footlocker rested next to a spindly rocker and a cracked and wavy cheval mirror.

Julie squatted next to the footlocker and tugged on the rusted padlock.

"Step back and let me get that for you," Tyler offered.

She stepped back. "You'll need bolt cutters to…"

He slammed the heel of his booted foot against the lock and it flew open. Julie looked duly impressed.

"Army," he said. "We get the job done, almost as well as investigative reporters."

A minute later, she was delving into the metal box as if it were a treasure chest. Unfortunately, there were enough remnants from the murdered woman's past to enthrall Julie for hours.

Tyler grew bored after she'd pulled the second nubby sweater from the metal box. He shuffled and then went to stare out the window.

"Why don't you take a coffee break in the fresh air?" Julie suggested, obviously noting his restlessness.

"I think I will."

"Take your time. I'll be awhile."

For once he totally believed her.

WITH TYLER GONE, JULIE settled in front of the locker, more positive than ever that she was doing the right thing. She'd doubted herself and her decision when she'd first walked into the house this morning. Even the walls had seemed like sinister eyes, watching and waiting for her to run like the menacing rat and threatened spider had.

But the attic seemed safer, more confined and now filled with secrets from so long ago. All she had to do was find the right combination of puzzle pieces to solve the crime.

Reaching into the stack of clothing, she pulled out a denim jacket studded with rhinestones and with the words *Lone Star* embroidered across the back. She held it up to her chest. The arms were too long and the stretch over her breasts would be tight, but she could wear it.

Not that she would.

She'd neared the bottom of the locker before her fingers sank into the soft body of a baby doll. Julie pulled it out and studied it. Worn. Frayed. The buttons missing from its dress.

Tears burned at the back of Julie's eyelids as she slipped the small doll into one of the plastic bags and placed it in the tote. From its appearance, Julie judged the doll to be much older than she was. No doubt a beloved relic from Muriel's childhood.

Next, she pulled out a floor-length red broomstick skirt with exquisite detail. The fabric appeared to be a nubby silk and linen. Tiny bluebonnets were embroidered into the waistband.

Even at prices eighteen years ago, the skirt must have cost a fortune. Julie refolded it carefully and set it next to the doll.

Diving back into what had become a treasure chest, she discovered two framed pictures. She lifted them carefully.

They were both of Muriel Frost as a teenager—one in a cheerleading outfit, one in a cap and gown and holding a high-school diploma. Slid in between them was an unframed snapshot, also of Muriel Frost but when she was years older, perhaps close to the time she'd been murdered.

Julie held it up and shifted so that she could capture all the light offered by the dingy window.

Muriel was wearing the red broomstick skirt and a white peasant blouse. Her dusty blond hair was piled on top of her head and curly wisps danced about her blushed cheeks. A smile parted full lips as red as the skirt. She looked absolutely stunning.

A man had been in the picture originally. His arm resting around Muriel's shoulder offered proof of his presence, even though the rest of him had been ripped away.

Julie's pulse skyrocketed. There was nothing that screamed a breakup like a man being torn from the picture, especially when Kara had said that Muriel hadn't been serious about anyone since she'd started working with her. That had been two years before the murder.

This could be her first real clue, but she needed the other half of the picture. Her fingers ripped through the remaining clothes until her nails scratched across the metal bottom of the locker.

"Julie."

Tyler's call startled her.

"What is it?" she yelled, her voice echoing around her.

"Come down here for a minute, will you? I think I may have found something useful."

"I'll be right there." She started to leave things as they were, but hesitated. Moving quickly, she sealed the torn picture and the red skirt in separate plastic bags and shoved them into the tote. The bag bounced comfortingly against her hip as she raced down the staircase.

Tyler was standing behind the rolltop desk on the second floor, holding what looked like a page torn from a checkbook register. "The checks are dated from February 17 through April 14, exactly eighteen years ago."

Excitement gurgled inside Julie like a fast-flowing brook. Muriel had been killed on April 16. "Let me see."

He handed it to her. "You should probably turn this over to the local sheriff once you've taken a look at it."

"The sheriff had eighteen years to find evidence. This is staying with me."

The hum of an engine and the crackle of tires on gravel interrupted the conversation. "Sounds like we have company," Tyler said, walking over to the window. "In a squad car."

Cripes! Julie took the wrinkled page from the check ledger and buried it in her bra. She took the picture with the missing man from the tote, unzipped her shorts and stuffed it inside her panties. She was all too aware of

Tyler's eyes on her while she did, but it was the only guaranteed safe hiding place she could think of.

They reached the living room just as the front door opened. A burly, whiskered man with a square, ruddy face stepped inside.

"What the hell are you doing in here?" he demanded.

Julie glared back at him. "Who wants to know?"

"Sheriff Caleb Grayson, that's who. And you two are trespassing." He rested his hand on the butt of his weapon.

"And let me guess," Tyler said. "You shoot trespassers around here."

"Just the smart asses who give me a reason. Let's see your ID."

Tyler fished his from his pocket while Julie stressed out trying to decide how to smuggle her tote bag to her car without the sheriff taking it from her.

Sheriff Grayson huffed and then smacked his lips as if he were eating chocolate. "Tyler Ledger. The murderer's kid. Now isn't that interesting?" He turned to Julie. "And I guess that would make you Julie Gillespie."

"That would be me."

The sheriff snorted. "You don't listen too well, do you?"

"I listen," she said. "I'm just not intimidated by you. I know my rights as a citizen."

"They don't extend to breaking and entering. What's in that tote bag you're hugging so hard?"

"Personal items," she lied.

"Let's have a look."

"She said it's personal," Tyler said. His muscles bunched and flexed.

A fight was not what Julie needed, at least not over a doll and a long red skirt. She handed the bag to the sheriff.

He checked it out and chuckled. "Yep. You know your stuff. Worthless clothes and toys. Ought to keep you around just for laughs. But I'm not."

He tossed the bag to the floor instead of giving it back to her. "Get out of my county or I'll arrest you on general principles. Is that clear?"

"Not to me," Tyler said. "I kind of had the idea I'd been over in the Middle East fighting for the home of the brave and the free."

The sheriff's ruddy face got redder and his hand went back to the butt of his gun.

"Perfectly clear to me," Julie said, grabbing Tyler's arm and pulling him toward the door.

"Glad you've come to your senses." The sheriff dusted his hands as if he were through with her. His cell phone rang and he turned and walked away a few steps before answering.

Julie grabbed her tote bag. "Now it's time to go," she urged as she exited the house and made a run for it before the sheriff decided to pat her down and discover she was leaving with more than the skirt and doll.

Tyler jogged to the car. "I'm starting to see why you enjoy this line of work."

IT WAS THREE IN THE AFTERNOON when Julie pulled out of Garfield's Garage and Car Wash, the best that

Mustang Run had to offer according to Troy Ledger. Sans mud, her white Ford was recognizable again.

Pete Garfield, evidently a friend of Troy's, had also balanced her tires as a favor since some jerk had run her off the road and kept going. Just wanted to show her that not all Texans were so inhospitable, he'd claimed.

He'd also suggested she let him smooth the dent in her bumper one day next week. He didn't mention free, though, so she thanked him and assured him that she could live with a minor flaw.

Julie started back to the Willow Creek Ranch, then changed her mind and turned toward the older section of the small town. She might as well do some exploring while she was out on her own.

Tyler had wanted to come with her, but she'd balked. She did not want or need a bodyguard, especially since it was evident to her that Sheriff Grayson was behind the original threat. His growl was no doubt a lot worse than his bite.

Besides, she needed time alone to think about the events of the morning. Tyler made it difficult to think. Not that it was his fault, but whenever he was near, her senses reeled with the essence of him. The sensation was unfamiliar and disturbing on every level.

In a way it was nice to have someone actually worry about her and fret over her safety, albeit a man who clearly didn't trust her. It seemed a lifetime ago since she'd been on anyone's priority list.

She loved his humor, the way he kept even serious matters from becoming unnecessarily oppressive. The way he looked at her like she was the whipped cream for his sundae was completely intoxicating.

But she wasn't fooled for a second. He might find her tempting, but she was his diversion, an escape from dealing with the father he'd supposedly come thousands of miles to see.

Hopefully the two of them were making progress today, which was another reason he shouldn't be here with her. Dylan had insisted Tyler take a ride around the ranch with him and Troy so that he could see all the improvements they'd made. Troy had invited her, as well, but she'd politely declined.

Julie turned onto a two-lane street with angled parking and cafés and shops on either side. They all looked as if they'd been built decades ago and had remained untouched by time. Not a chain store in the bunch.

The street sign read Main Street.

The light at the end of the next block turned from yellow to red and she slowed to a stop as a young couple pushing a stroller crossed in front of her. The man said something to the woman and her laughter drifted through the open car window.

Julie's gaze shifted to the sidewalk where pedestrians were strolling leisurely, as if they had all the time in the world. Two teenagers with book packs, each with a cell phone attached to their ears like giant black moles, ducked into a sporting goods store.

A mother carrying a large shopping bag walking beside a young boy licking a double dip ice cream cone stopped to talk to an attractive lady in red shorts who'd just stepped out of a flower shop.

An elderly man in denim coveralls was holding the door of a small café for a stooped gray-haired woman pushing a walker. The woman's lips were moving a mile a minute as she pointed to the specials listed on a sandwich board outside the door. The man noticed Julie staring at him and waved.

Out of the blue, Julie experienced a weird sinking feeling, as if she'd dropped down the rabbit hole into a world that only existed in fiction. The sky was too blue. The air too clean. The antique street lamps too charming.

A town with roots, history, continuity—all things she'd never known.

The light turned green and she eased through the intersection and pulled into a parking place. She felt suddenly woozy and in need of a cup of black coffee.

Once parked she walked back to the café. Abby's Diner. The outside air was brisk but inside it was cozy and almost too warm. Julie shrugged out of her pink cardigan and scanned the booths, choosing one in the back.

The man and woman she'd seen enter both smiled and said good afternoon when she passed their booth. A cowboy who'd just delved into a slice of coconut pie piled high with meringue grinned and reached for his napkin to wipe the white froth from his mouth. Other patrons smiled and nodded. Mustang Run was a very friendly town.

A pert young waitress with a thick Texas drawl stopped at her elbow almost as soon as she'd sat down. "Welcome to Abby's. What can I get you today?"

"Coffee. Black."

"Are you sure? Abby just took a pecan pie out of the oven."

"I'm certain it's delicious, but only the coffee for me."

"I'm supposed to offer everyone pie, but I figured that with your great figure, you didn't go in much for rich desserts."

Julie smiled. "Thank you, but I don't always resist temptation."

"I'm getting better at it," the waitress said, continuing the conversation even though the diner was crowded with people no doubt wanting their pie.

"The first week I worked here, I gained five pounds on the chocolate custard alone. The cowboy I was dating teased that I was going to outweigh his new heifer if I kept gaining. Now I limit myself to one slice a week."

"What happened to the boyfriend?"

"I dumped his sorry ass. Turned out he didn't have a heifer or even a job. Don't you just hate liars?"

"Unless the person has a very good reason for stretching the truth."

The waitress looked up as the bell over the door tinkled and a good-looking guy in jeans and a blue shirt walked in. She flushed with pleasure when he looked her way and promptly forgot all about Julie. She hurried back to the counter, hanging over it adoringly as she took the guy's order.

Julie opened her purse and pulled out the check register that Tyler had found. She'd looked at it briefly. Nothing had jumped out at her then, so now it was intense scrutiny time.

The murder had occurred in the spring, April 16, probably on a day much like this one when the Hill Country was bursting with new growth and the air was sweet with the fragrance of wildflowers.

By the time the waitress returned with the coffee, Julie was so into the register she barely noticed. She thanked her without looking up. She didn't want to encourage another conversation about liars.

She neared the end of the page. Check 1980 had been written to Kara Saunders on March 19 for $125. There was no notation as to what it was for.

Check 1985 had been written to Candice Cameron on April 1 for $186.00. If that amount was for rent, housing had definitely been a lot cheaper back then. And rent was usually rounded off to the nearest ten, at least Julie's had always been. Again no notation for what the check covered.

Julie stopped and took a sip of the coffee.

"How is it?"

She looked up to find a middle-aged woman with deep-set blue eyes, graying hair and a contagious smile leaning against the back of her booth. A slice of pecan pie dominated the saucer she was holding.

"The coffee is great, but I didn't order the pie."

"I know, but you look as if you need it. Too much scowl on your face. That makes wrinkles, you know."

"In that case, I'll probably need a face lift by the time I'm thirty," Julie said. "But I'll work on eliminating the scowl."

"I'm guessing you already work too hard," the woman said. "Anyway, the pie's on me, a treat to lift your spirits."

"I can't let you do that."

"I insist. I do it all the time with new customers. More often than not, it makes regulars of them." She slid the pie in front of Julie. "I'm Abby. Welcome to my diner."

"I'm Julie. It's nice to meet you, Abby."

"I'll bet you're in town for the bluebonnet festival," Abby said. "You have good hands. I always notice the customer's hands. I'll bet you're one of the artists here for the craft demonstrations." Abby put a finger to her chin as if thinking hard. "Let me guess. A potter?"

"No. Unfortunately, I have no artistic talents. I'm not even here for the festival."

"Here for work? Or to visit someone?"

"Both, but I hear the festival is entertaining and I do love the bluebonnets. I never realized they grew so thick or so blue."

"Some years are better than others. Have to get the right amounts of rain at the right time and get the temperature to cooperate. This year is just about perfect."

"Have you lived in Mustang Run long?" Julie asked.

"All my life. Wouldn't dream of livin' anywhere else, though I'd love to go to Rome one day. I'd like to see the Vatican and those Coliseum ruins. Now I best get back in the kitchen and check on those cherry pies I put in the oven."

Still she lingered. "You know if you can't take in the whole festival, you should at least go to the dance."

"Will you be there?" Julie asked.

"You better know it. It's the one night of the year I get to dance till I drop. I don't even feel bad about not having a partner. I have a lot more fun than those married women trying to drag their husbands onto the dance floor."

Julie sipped her coffee, though the sinking feeling that had prompted her stopping in had passed. Abby was better than caffeine, which probably explained why the diner was practically full in the middle of the afternoon. Well, that and the pies.

"I'll bet you have to fight the men off," Julie teased.

Abby chuckled. "Now wouldn't that be nice. But I've got my eye on one. I won't say who."

"I hope he likes pie."

"He likes it just fine, especially my buttermilk pie. You should see him gobble it down. Come to the dance and you just might meet him. And guaranteed you'll meet some cute cowboys who'll twirl you around until you're plumb dizzy."

"I doubt I can make it, but if I do, I'll look you up."

"You do that, and enjoy your pie."

"I will. Thanks."

The bell over the door tinkled again. This time a man with one good arm and a shirt sleeve that hung free below the elbow of the other sauntered in. He took off his hat and squeezed in at the counter.

Abby walked over and poked him on the shoulder.

"Well, if it's not old man Hartwell. What's the matter? Janie run you off and tell you to bother somebody else for a change?"

"Nope. I smelled pie clear down at the beauty shop. So cut me a slice, woman."

"Your usual?"

"Ain't no kind of pie but cherry in my book. You know that."

"Cherry pie, coming up."

Julie went back to the ledger. Her gaze fastened immediately on the name Zeke Hartwell, the same last name as the man who'd just ordered cherry pie. What were the chances of that?

It was almost like an omen. She looked back at the notation.

Check 1989, the last check Muriel Frost had ever written. The amount was $200 and the notation merely said repairs.

Julie finished the pie to the last crumb even though she hadn't been hungry. It was that good. She let the waitress refill her cup while she waited for Abby to reappear so she could ask her if she knew a Zeke Hartwell. For all she knew, it could be the one-armed man finishing his cherry pie.

After the second cup of coffee when there was still no Abby, Julie asked the waitress to see if the owner had a minute to answer a quick question.

"She's elbow deep in piecrust dough. But you can go on back to the kitchen." The young waitress nodded toward a door behind the counter. "Abby won't mind. That's her second home."

Julie paid her bill and pushed through the swinging door into a small, but organized kitchen. Abby was rolling circles of dough on a glistening white prep table.

"The pie was as good as promised," Julie said.

Abby glanced up, barely breaking her rhythmic rolling stroke. "Good, but something tells me you didn't come back here just to tell me that."

"You have good instincts."

"I reckon I do. Always have had. Sometimes it gets me in trouble. Mostly not."

"I was just wondering if you know a man named Zeke Hartwell. I think he might work as a handyman, or at least he used to."

Abby kept rolling dough. "What you got that needs fixing?"

"Nothing," Julie answered quickly. "A mutual friend just asked me to look Zeke up while I was in Mustang Run, but he wasn't sure Zeke still lived in the area."

"There are some Hartwells in Mustang Run. Tom Hartwell was in the restaurant a few minutes ago. You might have seen him. Tall. A little paunchy. Lost most of one arm a few years back in a hay-baling accident. I've never met a Zeke Hartwell."

"Does Tom have relatives in the area?"

"He has a brother who used to visit sometime. If I remember correctly, Tom's wife Janie didn't care for him much. And that's odd. Janie likes 'bout nearly everybody. She has a beauty shop in the next block. Janie's Shears. You could stop by there and ask her if there's a Zeke in the Hartwell clan."

"Good idea."

"Sometimes she closes early if business gets slow, but if you don't catch her today, she'll be open again tomorrow."

"Thanks, Abby. I'll hurry and see if I can catch her."

It wasn't much to go on, but at least a Zeke Hartwell who was working for Muriel Frost at an isolated farmhouse was a credible lead.

Julie's optimistic attitude hit a roadblock ten minutes later when the cardboard sign hanging on the door of Janie's Shears had been turned to closed. She knocked anyway, hoping Janie Hartwell might still be in the back of the shop and come to the door. No luck.

She'd just have to wait one more day. But she would follow up. She wondered if the sheriff had questioned Zeke, or if he was one of the local good old boys who'd slipped under the radar.

She was so deep in thought that she practically ran into Collette rushing out of a small boutique on the corner near where she'd parked.

"Julie," Collette said. "I didn't know you were coming into town this afternoon. We could have ridden in together. You are still staying at the ranch, aren't you?"

"I'm still there," she said, knowing Collette was hoping for a different answer.

Collette scanned the area. "Is Tyler with you?"

"No. Why would he be?"

"No reason." Collette held up her package. "I found a great pair of sandals for the dance Thursday night, snazzy, but comfortable. Since I'm the official photographer, I'll probably never get to sit down."

Okay, Collette was making a stab at being friendly. And who could blame her that she didn't like having a reporter on the ranch? The least Julie could do was sound interested in the festival.

"I stopped in Abby's Diner for pie and coffee," she said. "Abby told me what a great time I'd miss if I didn't attend the dance."

Collette waved at a guy who honked when he drove by them. "Don't you just love Abby?" she said.

"Yes. She's delightful."

"I think she has a crush on Troy."

"Is buttermilk pie his favorite?" Julie asked.

"It is if Abby's doing the baking."

"Then I think you may be right about the crush."

"I better be going," Collette said. "But if there's anything you need to know about Mustang Run, just ask. I've lived here all my life, though I probably don't know nearly as much about what's going on around here as Abby does."

"There is one thing," Julie said. "Do you know a man named Tom Hartwell? His wife owns Janie's Shears."

"Sure, Janie cuts my hair. Why?"

"Do you know if he has a brother named Zeke?"

Collette toyed with a stray curl, her expression signaling her inability to speak with confidence. "Janie's from a large family, but I've never heard them mention Tom having a brother. Sorry."

"That's okay. I'll wait and ask Janie tomorrow."

"Does Zeke Hartwell have something to do with your investigation?"

"Possibly."

"Well, good luck. Gotta run. Dylan will be looking for me."

Happiness radiated from Collette when she merely uttered Dylan's name. Julie wondered if she knew how lucky she was.

Suddenly, all Julie could think of was dancing in Tyler's arms to a Western band beneath bright Texas stars. She stared into the window of the boutique. One of the shop's super slim mannequins was dressed in a revealing black sundress accented by a sparkling belt. The other was draped in a multitiered blue broomstick skirt and white peasant blouse that looked so much like the one Muriel had on in the torn picture that Julie's heart skipped a beat.

Acting impulsively, she walked in and bought the blouse in a size small without even trying it on. Fortunately, it wasn't expensive, since it wasn't her style. She'd probably never wear it.

But somehow buying it seemed right.

After the rash purchase, she walked back to the car, amazed at how ready she was to return to Willow Creek Ranch. She'd like to go over the information about Zeke with Troy and see if he knew anything about him.

Mostly she wanted to see Tyler. Foolish, she knew, but she'd missed him every minute she'd been gone.

She had opened the car door and was about to slide behind the wheel when she noticed the large envelope tucked beneath the windshield wiper. Her mood plunged.

Surely not another threatening note.

She tore it open and reached inside. Gasping, the contents slipped though her shaky fingers as her blood rushed to her brain in dizzying, frigid waves.

Chapter Six

Tyler stared at the picture that Julie had dropped to the table in front of him. A woman's nude and bloodied body was stretched across the floor, her brains spilling from an open bullet wound, no doubt delivered from close range.

For one sickening instant, he thought it was a picture of his mother and his heart felt as if someone were scraping across it with rusty nails. But the dead woman was a blonde. His mother's hair had been dark as night.

"Where did you get this?"

"It was left on my windshield while I was having coffee in Mustang Run." Her voice shook with anger and a vulnerability that surprised him.

Tyler's protective instincts kicked in and every muscle in his body tightened. It was all he could do not to bury his fist in the wall for lack of a better target.

"This was delivered with it." She pulled a note from a brown envelope lying next to the picture.

Stay out of this, or you'll be next.

"Son of a bitch. When I get my hands on that arrogant quack of a sheriff, I'll…"

"But what if the sheriff isn't the one trying to frighten me off," she whispered. "What if it's the killer?"

Tyler muttered a string of curses. Why had he not even considered the obvious? That changed the complexion of everything and upped the danger quotient to deadly. And he'd let Julie go into town alone.

"I'll take care of this," he said, spitting his words through clenched teeth.

"No one can take care of anything until we find the killer."

Her voice dissolved in a shudder. Tyler pulled Julie into his arms. She trembled and burrowed her head against his chest. His chin rested on the top of her head and he could feel the rapid beating of her heart as her body pressed against his.

Tremors of desire rocked though him. It wasn't the time or the place and he struggled to tamp down the need that had erupted inside him. It had been eons since a woman had affected him the way Julie did—if ever.

Fortunately, he knew his limitations, knew he was poison where relationships were concerned. He simply wasn't a twosome kind of person.

But he would not stand by and let some maniac torture Julie like this.

Tyler had faced the best and worst of humanity over the last four years. He'd watched a young soldier face enemy fire head-on to pull his injured buddy to safety. Both had died that day, their sweat, blood and tears intermingled with their mangled bodies. He knew valor. He knew depravity.

And whoever had left that nauseating, repulsive

photograph for Julie to find was a sorry, sick, dangerous bastard.

Footsteps sounded on the back steps. Julie jerked
away from him abruptly as if they were teenagers who'd
been caught making out.

The picture was lying in full view on the kitchen
table when Troy stepped into the room.

"How was…" Troy stopped midsentence and Tyler
could tell from the pasty hue of his skin that he'd had
the same instant flashback that Tyler had experienced.

He revived quickly and walked to the edge of the
table for a closer look. "Is that Muriel Frost?"

"Yes." Julie's voice was strained but she seemed to
have regained some of her composure.

Troy worried the jagged scar that ran down his right
cheek. "Did Sheriff Grayson give that to you?"

"I'm not sure. If he did, it was done anonymously and
not meant to be helpful." She explained how it came to
be in her possession and then showed Troy the note.

"So much for the law being on the side of the citizens.
Not that the sheriff's being a conniving rat surprises
me," Troy declared.

"There's no proof the sheriff left it for her," Tyler
said, though he'd jumped to that same conclusion.

"That's a police photograph," Troy insisted. "No one
else would have had the opportunity to photograph the
victim in that condition. The police would have covered
her up as soon as the crime scene was secure, if not
before."

"The killer would have all the opportunity he
needed," Julie said.

Troy looked doubtful. "Why would the killer hold on to such an incriminating piece of evidence?"

"They say serial killers frequently keep a souvenir from their murders," Tyler said. "Maybe the Frost woman's killer kept photographs."

"One theory expounded by the press was that Muriel was murdered by a serial killer," Julie said. "Someone who staked out his victims and knew that Muriel Frost lived in an isolated area. He killed for pleasure or because he felt driven to. That would explain why nothing appeared to be missing from the house, not even the cash that was in her handbag."

Troy paced. "The serial killer theory was never proved."

"But it makes sense," Tyler said. "And that same serial killer just might have found his way to the Willow Creek Ranch." He was beginning to see why Julie felt so strongly that the two murders could be connected. Of course, the serial killer theory also ruled out Troy as Helene's killer, which made it surprising that Troy wasn't backing the possibility all the way.

"You stated that the niece witnessed the Frost murder," Tyler said. "Did she give a description to the police?"

"Not according to the reports I read," Troy said. "They all said she was so traumatized that she didn't remember anything. She didn't speak for days after and never answered any questions."

Julie picked up the photograph and held it to the light. "I just noticed that there's a person's shadow in this picture. See." She moved closer to Tyler and traced a dark spot along the edge of the photograph.

"It looks to be a person, all right," Tyler agreed, "but I can't tell if it's a man or a woman."

"If it was a serial killer, then it's almost certain the killer was a man," Troy said. "But I still think Grayson or one of his deputies left that picture on your car. He warned you to stay out of this and he's just the type of macho law officer to put some teeth into the threat."

"We can stand here all day and throw around assumptions," Tyler said. "But the only thing we know for certain is that someone is going to cause a lot of trouble if Julie continues on this case."

Julie dropped the photo back to the table. "What's your point, Tyler?"

She wasn't going to like the point. If he were going to stay in Mustang Run to look out for her, he might see it differently. But he'd taken his time getting down to Texas and now he had just a little over a week before he had to be back in Afghanistan and ready for duty.

He worked to keep his tone nonconfrontational. "Why not cut your teeth on an easier case, Julie, one where you don't attract threats, lunatic sheriffs and depraved madmen?"

Her eyes shot daggers at him. "You mean why don't I give up and go back to telling teenage girls how to dump a loser. Is that all you think I'm capable of, Tyler?"

"I never said that. But you're starting with basically no experience in this type of work. You can surely find an easier case than this to prove yourself."

Her hands flew to her hips. "I worked the New Orleans investigation."

She might be short on experience, but she for damn sure had no scarcity in the fire and passion departments. He was sure those were admirable traits in a reporter. But that might not be enough to keep her alive.

"What's so important about this case?" he demanded. "Tell me why some woman who was killed eighteen years ago in a rural area in the Texas Hill Country is worth risking your life over?"

"Muriel Frost may be a nobody in the eyes of lots of people, but she was a living, breathing human and she deserves justice. I started this, Tyler, and I will finish it. But I can leave this ranch now if this is inconveniencing you."

"Are you going to bring that up every time we have a disagreement?"

"Settle down, you two," Troy said. "You're not solving anything this way. Tyler, why don't you take Julie to see that new colt we checked out a few minutes ago? Your momma used to say there was nothing like a new baby or a just-born colt to put things in perspective."

His mother. How dare Troy talk about her like…

Like she'd mattered to him. Like he'd loved her.

How dare he? Unless he really was innocent.

"I've never seen a newborn colt," Julie said, backing away from the fury that had driven her only seconds before. "And I could use some perspective and time to cool down."

Tyler needed to escape this room and the tension

that was exploding inside his skull. "Then let's get out of here." He reached over and took Julie's hand in his.

Hers was cold, or else his was too warm. The hunger for her stirred deep inside him as they fell into step beside one another and took the worn path to the horse barn.

He wondered how long he'd be able to fight the attraction that grew stronger with every touch. And wondered how in hell he could get this turned on by a woman he had to fight so hard just to keep her safe.

FOR JULIE, IT WAS LOVE AT first sight. She perched on the bottom slat and leaned over the half door for a better look at the spindly legged colt with the deep brown eyes. Its coat was soft brown with specks of white on its nose and legs. The mother stood over it and kept a wary eye on the strangers who'd invaded her space.

"It's adorable. Does it have a name yet?"

"Yes. Guinevere. Dylan said Collette had the name picked out for weeks—just in case it was female."

"I love it. And you look like royalty, don't you, Guinie? You have such beautiful eyes," she cooed.

Tyler reached over and gave the watchful new mother some soothing strokes. "You've got a beautiful baby, Lady. Heard she came into the world fighting."

The gentle mare stepped closer and nestled her nose against Tyler's shirt. Julie stepped back.

"Have you been around horses much?" Tyler asked.

"Never. This is as close as I've ever been to one

except for when the police rode them for crowd control during Mardi Gras. I stayed well out of their way."

"We should go riding while you're here."

"Me, on top of one of those gigantic creatures? I don't think so."

"You'd like riding once you got the hang of it."

"Maybe, but I have no plans to find out."

"You're not afraid of death threats, but you're terrified of going horseback riding. You stamp around a house full of rats and scorpions, but you panic over a few longhorn cattle trying to get to the greener grass on the other side of the fence. You're a hard one to figure, Julie Gillespie."

"Let's not talk about murder in here," she said. "It spoils the atmosphere."

She leaned against an empty stall and soaked up the sounds and smells, as unfamiliar to her as the streets of Mustang Run had been. The odors were pungent—hay, horseflesh, leather from the adjoining tack room.

The sounds were strange, as well. Restless pawing of hooves on the hard earth beneath the hay. Breathy snorts. Arrhythmic neighs and whinnies. The whispery swish of luxurious tails.

The peculiarities wrapped around her, transporting her to a mystical place where life felt safe and secure, even for the animals. Only it hadn't been safe on this ranch for Helene Ledger. And not for Tyler, either. It must have been horrifying for him to be ripped from this peaceful environment and separated from all the people he loved.

She studied his profile, marveling at his masculinity

and the way he looked so natural in this setting. Looks were deceiving. When he was with Troy, the air crackled with tension.

Yet Tyler must have hoped to find some common ground between them when he'd come home to Mustang Run. She hesitated to bring up his past when she hated her own. But they were alone now and she found herself wanting to know and understand everything about him.

"How old were you when your mother died?" she asked.

"Not died. Murdered." He stepped away from the stall where Guinevere had started sucking at her mother's teat. "I was eight."

"It must have been a devastating time for you, losing both parents and your brothers."

"How did you know I was separated from my brothers?"

"Eve mentioned it the other night."

"I didn't quite lose all the family. I had Aunt Sibley." Tyler turned to face her and propped his right foot behind him, hooking the heel of his boot on one of the slats.

"Is she the one who raised you?"

"Yep, she was the unlucky one who had to take on the rambunctious eight-year-old."

"What was it like adjusting to a new life in an unfamiliar environment?"

Tyler shrugged. "It was life. She cooked and cleaned. I went to school. She took me to the doctor when I was sick and saw that I had everything I needed. She wasn't big on buying toys or letting me have friends over. What about you?"

"I was spoiled rotten. No siblings, and my parents doted on me." Odd how the lie felt bitter this time when normally she didn't give it a thought. She pulled her arms tight as if the scars and bruises from so long ago would swell and fester again if she exposed them to honesty.

"Did you ride horses when you were growing up?" she asked, changing the subject back to Tyler.

"No. I didn't start riding again until I went to college."

"In Texas?"

"In Bowling Green, Kentucky. I grew up just north of there, after leaving here. The grandfather of one of the guys in my college fraternity had a few horses and we went there about once a month and rode when we weren't hanging out at the lake. I guess it kind of sparked my appreciation of wide open spaces."

"Did you ever think of taking up ranching yourself?"

"I considered it."

"Instead you joined the army."

He turned back to the nursing colt and she took that to mean she'd pushed the questioning too far. She went over and stood beside him, not so close they touched, but close enough that the warmth and thrill of him closed in around her.

"The army seemed safer than coming back to Texas," he admitted.

His voice was hoarse, almost distant, but he reached

over and let his fingers tangle in her hair. When she looked up, their eyes met. Desire vibrated through her. She couldn't swallow. Her legs grew weak.

"I was afraid that if I came back here, the past would claim my future."

"It will anyway, if you let it, Tyler. You can never give it that power."

He lowered his lips to hers. A thousand emotions came to life at once, churning inside her until she felt as if she were drowning in marshmallow-like clouds. She sucked in the elation as if it were the only thing keeping her alive. When he pulled away, she had to reach for the stall door to keep from losing her balance.

"We should go," she said and then hated that he might take that to mean she didn't like the kiss.

"Is that what you want?"

No, what she wanted was to lie down in the hay with him and make love until all the reasons she shouldn't were erased from her mind. But making love would only complicate the investigation. And falling for a man who'd be out of her life in a few days would break her heart.

"It's probably best—for now," she whispered.

Unless he kissed her again, and all her ability to reason melted like chocolate in a hot car.

He didn't. By the time they reached the house, he'd grown distant. She couldn't compete with the issues that separated him from his father.

"It's Sheriff Grayson," Candice said, holding her hand over the phone's mike. "He says it's urgent."

Guy groaned inwardly. When wasn't it urgent with that pompous blowhard? He picked up the martini he'd just poured, extra dry and dirty, the way he liked it, before taking the phone from his wife.

"Evening, Grayson. I suppose you have a very good reason for bothering me at home."

"I wouldn't call if I didn't."

That was a matter for debate, had Guy been in the mood to start an argument.

"We could have trouble," Grayson said.

"There is no *we*."

"Best hear me out before you go jumping to that conclusion."

"Okay. What is it you want now?"

"You had trespassers today out at the old farm-house."

Guy's corporation owned hundreds of houses, some rural, some in town. Nonetheless, he knew exactly which house the sheriff was referring to.

"More addicts?" Guy asked. "If so, arrest them or let them burn the damn place down. I don't really care."

"Burning the house down might not be such a bad idea. Wouldn't advise it now, though. It wasn't addicts out there today. It was a reporter and some macho-acting cowboy from over Mustang Run way that she's hooked up with."

Guy gulped down half the drink. "Who was the reporter?"

"No one you've ever heard of. Name's Julie Gillespie. She was writing fluff for the *Times-Picayune* until about four months ago. She accidentally got dragged into some big sex scandal and now she fancies herself as legitimate."

"And the cowboy?"

"Tyler Ledger."

"Surely not one of Troy Ledger's sons."

"Afraid so."

Guy finished the drink. "So this inexperienced reporter has enlisted the son of a killer to help her investigate the Frost case."

"Yep. Told you that she has no clue what she's doing. But don't worry. I can handle her. She won't stick around long."

Arrogant bastard. Had Guy known years ago that Caleb Grayson was as incompetent as he was crooked, he could have saved himself a lot of trouble and money.

"Make sure you handle this, Grayson. One slipup and there will be hell to pay—on both our parts."

"No one knows that better than me, Mr. Cameron."

Grayson rattled on a few more minutes, but Guy had quit listening to his jabber. It didn't matter. Either Grayson took care of the situation or Guy would. It was probably better if he did it himself.

When he finished the conversation, he fixed himself another martini. Then he walked back into the den. Candice was on the white sofa they'd had shipped from France. The caftan she was wearing was of the finest silk.

Candice wasn't beautiful, had never been, but surprisingly, she'd improved with age. Or with money.

She lowered the gossip magazine she was reading

and slid the diamond-studded reading glasses down her nose. "What did Sheriff Grayson want this time?"

"Just to tell me that there were crack addicts hanging out at the old farmhouse again."

"They're probably the only people not convinced the house is haunted and they don't pay rent. You still have it insured, don't you? It would be just our luck to have one of them fall through that rotting attic window and then sue us for damages."

"We have plenty of insurance and you can't really complain about our luck, Candice."

"I guess not. Thomas called today. He's decided not to go to Florida for spring break."

"Did he say why?"

"He's going to the Hamptons to meet Cecelia's parents."

Pangs of regret mixed with pleasure. He liked Cecelia and her family, but Guy hated to think he might lose his only son to the northeast. He'd been afraid of that when Thomas got accepted at Princeton, but he'd gone along with what Thomas wanted.

What was the use of making money if you couldn't squander it on your only son?

"Meet the parents weekend. That should be interesting," he said, and then let the subject drop.

Love and marriage. Those had been two of Guy's biggest mistakes in life. Hopefully, it wouldn't be that way for Thomas.

THE THREE OF THEM HAD DINNER at the kitchen table, a homemade chicken potpie that Troy said a friend had brought over that day. Women bringing casseroles was the traditional form of Southern courting among the middle-aged set, Julie had teased.

"Works for me," Troy said. "As long as they don't start setting two plates at the table while they're here."

Tyler didn't participate in the teasing. Even if it hadn't been about Troy and other women, he couldn't have joined in. He felt boxed in when Troy was around. There were too many lines he couldn't cross. Too many subjects he couldn't discuss. Too much bitterness bubbling just below the surface of the forced cordiality.

When he'd made the decision to come back to the ranch, he'd thought the emotions of the past were far behind him and that his resentment toward Troy had hardened over like dried cement. He figured he could just size up the situation and see if he had any desire to fit into this "new" Ledger family. He fully expected that he wouldn't.

But now that he was here, the tension between him and the man he'd once idolized was impenetrable. It would remain that way unless Tyler reached the point where he was actually convinced Troy was innocent of killing Tyler's mother. He didn't see how that could happen when merely talking to Troy made him feel like a traitor to his mother, to his dead grandparents and even to acidic Aunt Sibley.

The only thing keeping Tyler at Willow Creek Ranch was Julie. She was the sunshine in what would have been nothing but storm clouds from dawn to dusk. Only now that he'd kissed her, he had no clear sense of where things should go from here. He had nothing to offer but protection, and Julie didn't seem to want that.

Yet, the kiss had been practically climactic, and a kiss like that required two parties who were feeling a lot more than the wind blowing.

The sound of an approaching car engine interrupted his thoughts and the banter between Troy and Julie.

"Are either of you expecting anyone?" Troy asked.

When they said no, Troy stood and walked into the living room so he could see who'd stopped in front of the house.

"It's just Bob Adkins," Troy said, once he'd checked. "I figured he'd be coming around to see you."

"Bob Adkins? Isn't that the man whose fence Julie plowed into?"

"That's the one."

"Then he's probably here to see me," Julie said, "wanting payment for damages."

"Money to reset a fence post? Never. Not Bob. He's more likely to apologize for sticking it your way."

"Go with him," Julie insisted of Tyler after Troy walked out of the kitchen to let Bob in. "You two visit in the living room. I'll make a pot of decaf coffee and clean off the table."

Tyler stood and started gathering plates. "Wouldn't you rather have me help you?"

"I don't need help." She took the plates from him with one hand and gave him a shove with the other. "Now, go."

"Well, look at you," Bob said when Tyler joined them.

"You turned into a man since I seen you last. And I hear you're in the army, serving in the Middle East."

"Yes, sir." Tyler extended a hand.

Bob ignored it and gave him a couple solid pats on the back in a kind of half hug. "Your momma would be real proud of you."

If she were alive.

"Bob bought us some venison sausage," Troy said, holding up a package swathed in freezer wrap.

"I figured you might enjoy a meal you can't get in the mess hall."

"I appreciate that."

"Yeah, it's real thoughtful of you to bring it by," Troy said.

"No trouble. Ruby Nelle's after me to get the freezer cleaned out anyway. Says she has to make room for her peaches and all them purple hull peas she's gonna make me shell this summer."

"How's she doing?" Troy asked.

"Doing good, 'cept for the arthritis. Not that a few pains will keep her from making me dance at the festival come Thursday. You two are going, aren't you?"

"Tyler might. I seriously doubt I'll make it," Troy said.

"You might want to reconsider, if for nothing else than to see the local politicians putting on their show. I guess you heard about State Senator Foley."

Troy set the package of venison on the mantel. "Can't say that I have. What's he done now?"

"He announced he's running for governor."

"That's odd. Ruthanne dropped off a chicken potpie this afternoon and she didn't mention it."

"You better watch that woman," Troy said. "She's so full of herself, she can't eat but one meal a day."

"Who's Ruthanne?" Tyler asked.

"The senator's ex-wife," Bob said. "Now she's busy keeping Austin plastic surgeons rich."

"Ruthanne was one of your mother's best friends," Troy added for Tyler's benefit.

"Yet she testified against Troy at his trial."

Tyler hadn't noticed that Julie had stepped into the family room until she got his attention with that comment. Now everyone had turned her way.

"You can't really hold that against Ruthanne," Troy said. "She just jumped on the bandwagon with everybody else."

"Not everybody," Bob reminded him. "And lying under oath is not exactly *just* following the other ducks into the pond."

"What did she testify?" Tyler asked, suddenly more curious than he wanted to be.

Julie stepped over to the hearth. "Ruthanne said under oath that she popped in the morning of the murder and found Helene furiously packing her luggage. When Ruthanne asked her where she was going, Helene said she was driving to her parents' house that afternoon. Helene told her that things had gone on long enough."

"What things?" Tyler asked.

"Ruthanne said she wasn't sure."

"If Helene actually said that, she was most likely

talking about her parents trying to interfere in our lives," Troy said.

Bob grunted and scratched a spot behind his ear. "The way Ruthanne told it, it was like the problems were between Troy and Helene."

Tyler hadn't remembered problems between his parents, but he'd been only eight. "Were problems that bad?"

Troy shoved his hands into the front pockets of his jeans in what appeared to be an act of frustration. "We had some money issues, but it was nothing serious. Your mother loved me and she was devoted to you boys. We had the future all planned. She knew how much I loved her. She *always* knew that."

"But her bags were packed," Julie said. "And that gave credence to Ruthanne's testimony and the prosecutor's case."

Tyler felt as if he'd swallowed rocks and that they were grinding to sand in his stomach. He couldn't even bear to look at Troy.

It suddenly struck him how much Julie knew about Troy's trial. An exposé covering two murders would be much more provocative than if it only covered one. Had that been her plan all along? Was that why she couldn't give up this investigation no matter how dangerous it became for her?

Succeed at any price, even if it involved moving in with a convicted killer and ignoring threats on your life.

Even if it meant lying in one breath and kissing the next.

Tyler heard the introductions taking place in the

background, but found it difficult to focus on the mundane.

"An investigative reporter." Bob repeated the words from the introduction as if they were so disgusting he had to spit them out of his mouth. "Don't go stirring up trouble for Troy. He don't deserve it. He and Helene were as in love as two people can get. Everybody knew that including that two-faced Ruthanne."

"Then I can't possibly make trouble for Troy," Julie said. "I'm only looking for the truth."

"All I'm saying is it's best to let sleeping dogs lie. Rile one and he's just liable to take a bite out of you."

Julie's cell phone rang. She took it out and checked the screen. "Excuse me, but I need to take this. Nice to have met you, Bob. And don't worry. I'm only collaborating with Troy, not investigating him."

Julie walked away. "I wouldn't trust her," Bob said.

"I invited her to stay here," Troy said, "and I plan to give her any help I can."

"You're too gullible, Troy. Trusting people you ought not trust is what landed you in prison in the first place. You thought being innocent was enough."

"I'm not that foolish anymore," Troy said. "Not after what I've been through and put my boys through. But there's a chance that Julie's investigation will bring me closer to finding Helene's killer."

"So you'll knowingly let this reporter drag up your past, as well?" Bob argued.

"If it helps."

Bob shook his head. "I just hope you're not letting wasps in the outhouse."

"I can handle this," Troy assured him.

Tyler walked to the front door with the two men and thanked Bob again for the sausage. He tried to put it from his mind, but Bob's warnings about Julie wouldn't let go of him.

He left Bob and Troy talking on the porch, picked up the venison, carried it to the kitchen and found a spot for it on the second shelf of the refrigerator. When he didn't see Julie, he checked the back door. She was standing on the top step, staring into the darkness.

He joined her, though neither said a word.

Finally, Julie broke the silence. "Aren't you going to ask who was on the phone?"

"It's none of my business who you talk to."

"It was Sheriff Grayson."

Tyler's muscles clenched. "What did he want?"

"He wants to see me in his office first thing in the morning."

"Did he say why?"

"To turn over a copy of all the information from his files concerning the Frost murder investigation."

"Why the sudden change in attitude?" Tyler questioned.

"Maybe because it's public documentation to a case that has been closed for years."

Tyler doubted that was the real reason. "I'll go with you."

"The sheriff particularly specified that I was not to bring you."

"I could care less what the sheriff wants. I'm going.

If nothing else, it will show the sheriff that you can't be intimidated."

"Good point, but I don't want you to mention the picture and warning that were left on my car."

"I thought you weren't afraid of him."

"I'm not, but saying I was in danger would provide him with an excuse to thwart my investigation."

"That's possible. I'm not convinced that *he* would see it that way."

He should let go of this, but if he did his suspicions would prey on his mind and make the doubts worse. He sat on the top step and tugged Julie down to sit beside him.

"Level with me," he said.

Julie stared up at him from beneath her thick lashes and the moonlight gave a silvery glow to her eyes. "What is it?"

"Exactly what role does Troy play in your investigation?"

"Do we have to go over this again?"

"It would help."

"I am trying to find out if the same person who killed Helene could have killed Muriel Frost. Troy's done some research into Muriel Frost's murder for the very same reason. We both have a stake in finding the truth. There's no reason we shouldn't compare notes."

"You said you're not investigating Troy and yet you seem to have all the evidence against him on the tip of your tongue."

"So that's what this is about." She pulled herself up until she was sitting ramrod straight. "You think I'm trying to convict Troy all over again, only this time with the printed page instead of a trial. But it's not me who's trying to convict him, Tyler Ledger. It's you."

She stood and stormed away without giving him a chance to reply. Not that he could put up much of an argument. She could well be right.

But that didn't mean he'd let Julie go alone to see the sheriff.

CALEB GRAYSON ARRIVED AT HIS office at the Sheriff's Department at exactly ten minutes before eight the next morning. He stopped and made small talk with his secretary and then chatted at the coffee pot for several minutes with two of his detectives who were just going off duty. It had been a quiet night.

He planned to make damned sure it remained a quiet day. For eighteen years, no one had questioned the department's handling of the Frost murder investigation. Joel Emmons had been sheriff at the time, an outgoing Texas native who didn't take any garbage off anybody.

They'd interrogated suspects. The suspects had ironclad alibis. And the pathetic, stringy-haired niece who'd been in the house the whole time had never answered one question about the killer's appearance.

That information was all contained in the files that he planned to give Julie Gillespie, the same files that everyone else in the department had access to.

Caleb stretched back in his leather swivel chair and propped his feet on the desk, satisfied that he had everything under control, whether Julie dropped the investigation or not.

The best scenario was for her to examine the police file and then to decide the investigation had been thorough and that she didn't have a chance of milking a story out of this.

If she didn't drop it, well, then he'd do what he had to do to get her off the case.

Lucky for him, being the sheriff came with perks.

Chapter Seven

Tyler settled in a metal folding chair and sipped strong, black coffee from a foam cup. Julie sat next to him, in a matching metal folding chair except that unlike his, hers hadn't been dusted with crumbs and a sticky substance Tyler sincerely hoped had been edible at one time.

The sheriff had the power seat behind a chunky brown desk. He'd made a stab at being hospitable until he'd spotted Tyler. Then his whole demeanor had changed.

Grayson obviously had an agenda. Tyler didn't have it figured out as of yet, but there was no doubt the man did not like dealing with reporters, or with Tyler for that matter.

Once the clerk who'd served the coffee was gone, Grayson reached into his top desk drawer, pulled out a thick manila file and placed it on the desk in front of him. He stared at Julie as if she were a crook he expected to have to shoot at any minute.

"You said you worked alone," he said, turning only briefly to glare at Tyler.

"I usually do."

"Guess it's handy to have a new partner living and sleeping right there in the same house."

"We're here to pick up a file," Tyler said. "If we wanted a sermon, we'd have gone to church. And where Julie sleeps is none of your business."

"Who I give access to files is very much my business."

"We've already covered my credentials," Julie said. "So how about just handing over the file and we'll get out of your way."

"We need to set some ground rules first."

"We?" Tyler asked, not hiding the sarcasm. "What role does Julie get in that?"

The sheriff picked up a silver ballpoint pen and tapped it against a notepad. "Okay, *I* make the rules. *You* follow."

"Is that rule number one?" Tyler asked.

"You can give it whatever number you want. Just don't forget it. I don't want you interviewing any of my deputies while they're on the clock. They're here to do the county's work, not yours. If they want to talk to you on their time, that's their business."

Julie nodded. "I can live with that."

The sheriff leaned forward and steepled his fingers. "Don't harass the citizens of my county, especially the Camerons," he said, still nursing his condescending tone.

"The Camerons aren't on the county payroll," Tyler reminded him.

"No, but they've heard that you trespassed yesterday and they've requested that Miss Gillespie respect their property and their privacy. They cooperated fully in the original investigation. You can read accounts of that in the police file."

Julie crossed her shapely legs. "Muriel Frost was an employee of the Camerons. I'm sure they'd want to help find her killer in any way they could."

"You're not in law enforcement, Julie. You're in journalism. It's not a killer but a story and a career boost you're looking for. The Ledgers may be fooled. I'm not, and neither are the Camerons."

"How long have you been sheriff?" Tyler asked.

"Eleven years. I was a deputy ten years before that. So to answer your real question, yes, I was working for the department when Miss Frost was murdered."

Julie began to swing her leg in jerky, agitated movements. "Were you in on the original investigation?"

"As a matter of fact, I was the first officer to arrive on the scene and later was named the lead detective in the case."

Which made it a lot easier to understand why he didn't want the local and possibly the cable news stations to discover that the case had been bobbled.

And the first officer on the scene could have easily taken the picture left on Julie's windshield. It would be interesting to see if the original of that same picture was in the police file.

"The Frost murder was extremely brutal with no obvious motive," Julie said. "Isn't that very different from the types of murders you usually deal with in this area?"

"We've solved eighty percent of our homicides in the last five years. That's a damn good record for any agency."

"Yes, but you have far fewer homicides than some of the larger, more urban counties. The last murder in your county was a clear case of spousal abuse. The woman lived long enough to tell you who attacked her.

"In the one before that, the victim had been shot in a barroom brawl and there were dozens of witnesses. In the one before that, the victim was shot by a jealous husband who confessed while being interrogated."

"Are you going somewhere with this?"

"A murder without witnesses or obvious motives would be unusual for you even now. So you have to admit that it is possible that eighteen years ago, you may have overlooked a few clues that would have led to an arrest in the Frost murder."

The veins in Sheriff Grayson's neck bulged like a bungee cord and his jaw clenched so tightly it looked as if it might have to be pried open. Julie clearly had him on the ropes. No matter what came of her investigation, Tyler figured *Dear Julie* wouldn't be giving lovelorn puppy advice any longer.

The sheriff glanced at his watch. "I have a meeting in ten minutes. If you have questions, ask them—quickly." He shoved the file in front of him to the back edge of his desk. "Otherwise, take the information and get out of my way. I have legitimate work to do."

"Did you interrogate a man named Zeke Hartwell?"

"I don't have the case file memorized, but, yes, I believe we did. He did some repair work for Muriel Frost just before her murder if I'm remembering correctly."

"He was never arrested."

"Then I'm assuming we ruled him out as a suspect. I do remember that Betty Calhoun had an airtight alibi."

"Who's Betty Calhoun?" Tyler asked. He was pretty sure he hadn't heard Julie mention her name before.

"A woman who threatened to kill Muriel Frost if she caught her with her husband. Muriel Frost didn't have a stellar reputation, if you get my drift."

Julie stopped shaking her leg and planted both feet on the floor. "That doesn't mean she shouldn't receive justice."

"I never said that it did."

"Do either Zeke or Betty still live in the area?" Tyler asked.

"Zeke left as soon as we gave him clearance. Not that I blame him. Nobody was going to hire him as long as even the slightest suspicion hung over his head. Betty stuck around, but ended up divorcing her husband a couple years later."

"I'll pay her a visit," Julie said.

The sheriff stood and picked up the file. "Wouldn't advise it. She died two years ago of complications following surgery."

"What about Zeke Hartwell?" Julie asked. "Have you kept up with him?"

"No reason to. He could be anywhere." He handed Julie the file and walked to the door, opening it and standing back so they could walk past him.

"Thanks for the file," she said, "and for your time." She extended a hand. The jerk ignored it.

"If you're smart you'll move on to a case with

something to prove. This one's done and opening it up for your personal gain will backfire. You'll wish you were back spreading advice to pimple-faced brats."

So the sheriff had done some investigating of his own. Tyler went face-to-face with the pompous lawman. "That sounds like a threat."

"Take it any way you like."

Tyler fought an urge that would have landed him directly in the slammer and made it impossible to see that Julie stayed safe. He was beginning to suspect a conspiracy among people who didn't want the Frost case opened again.

If Muriel Frost's murderer was part of the scheme, he'd likely have no qualms about killing again, this time in order to remain a free man.

Tyler was facing a few challenges of his own. He had to find a way to keep Julie with him all the time and still keep his sensual urgings under control. Which meant he couldn't get his lips anywhere near hers.

The fun had just been banished from their relationship. Some vacation this would be.

As soon as Grayson was certain that Tyler Ledger and Julie Gillespie had left the building, he picked up the phone and punched in Candice Cameron's private number.

She should be home alone now. Guy went into the office by seven every morning. Candice dragged in whenever she chose, usually around ten, and then she took a two-hour lunch. Grayson found it useful to know such things.

He didn't fault Candice for giving herself generous leeway with her hours. A woman with her money didn't have to work at all, but she went into the office every day and knew pretty much everything that went on in their billion dollar business.

She deserved credit for that, though Grayson suspected her time spent in the office was in large part an attempt to keep an eye on Guy and protect her marriage and business interests.

He was about to give up when Candice finally picked up.

"Hello."

"Good morning, Candice. Hope I didn't interrupt anything important."

"I wouldn't have answered the phone if you had. Is there a problem, Sheriff?"

"You could say that, but it's nothing the two of us can't handle."

"What kind of problem?"

"It concerns the murder of Muriel Frost."

Grayson heard her gasp and imagined her eyes getting big and her ample breasts spilling out of a shimmery negligee. He'd always found Candice attractive, in a sleazy, overkill kind of way.

"What about the murder?" she asked, clearly distraught.

It was sinful how much he enjoyed toying with her mind this way. But it was necessary.

Grayson always did whatever was necessary to get the job done right.

That's what made him the perfect sheriff. That and

the fact that he stayed on top of things. You load the gun before you run into the rattlesnake. Julie Gillespie had best watch where she slithered.

JULIE BURIED HERSELF IN HER copy of the police file the minute they reached the car. She did a quick search for the photo she'd received yesterday. When she didn't find it, an uneasy feeling seeped inside her and started crawling along her nerve endings.

"Either Sheriff Grayson chose not to include the crime scene photo we've already seen, or else it was never part of the file."

"Did he include any photos?"

"Yes, just not that one."

"If it was originally part of the file, he probably removed it to cover his tracks."

"At this point, I hope that's the case. I'd much rather receive threats from Grayson than from Muriel's killer."

"Is there anything on Zeke Hartwell in the file?"

"Yes." She scanned until she found his name again. "Zeke was questioned and then released. He remained a possible suspect until his alibi checked out."

"What was it?"

"He said he was working on Leanne Crier's house that day. She vowed he didn't leave the job all day."

"I doubt the woman stood there and watched him from sunup to sundown."

"Grayson bought her testimony and apparently so did Sheriff Emmons. Zeke was questioned a couple times after that, but he came in willingly and was never arrested."

"Was there a lie detector test?"

"Wait. Let me see if I can find that." She scanned farther. "Here it is. It says that he was voluntarily tested and that he passed." She thumbed through to the back of the file. "They included official test documentation on two other people, but not on Zeke."

"Who else was tested?"

"Kara Saunders. She never mentioned that. And Betty Calhoun. I never saw anything about her in any of the articles I read."

They rode in silence for at least half an hour while she scrutinized every page.

"I could use some coffee," Tyler said.

She looked up as he slowed and pulled into a parking spot. She'd been so lost in the file's gore, she hadn't noticed that they'd pulled off the highway.

"Where are we?"

"Bandera, Texas. We're taking the long way home."

"Isn't this where your brother Sean and his family live?"

"Yes, but their horse farm is about five miles out of town."

"He won't like it that you've come so close and not stopped in to see him."

"I promised I'd drive over on Friday so Sean can show me his place."

"Sounds like a real family fun day."

"It would be, if I felt like family."

"You will. It just takes time."

"Maybe."

He didn't sound convinced. And, now, when he should be bonding with his brothers and his dad, he was with her, yet again. Her timing in arriving at Mustang Run couldn't have been worse for him.

Timing. It was everything when you thought about it. It had put her in the right place at the right time in New Orleans. It had run her off the road just in time to be rescued by the most seductively fascinating man she'd ever met. But timing seemed too circumstantial to explain everything.

"Do you believe in serendipity, Tyler?"

"I never gave it much thought." And it was clearly not something he wanted to discuss.

He opened his car door and came around to open hers while she carefully slipped every page back into the file. She dropped the whole file into a blue canvas messenger bag and slung it over her shoulder. No way was she leaving it in the car. It was only copies of the original reports but if anything happened to it, she was pretty sure the sheriff would not replace it.

The ambiance caught her by surprise as she stepped from the car and looked around. "What an interesting place. I feel like I've been traveling through time and dropped into the Old West. Look, there's two horses tied to a hitching post."

"I guess that sign says it all."

Julie looked where Tyler was pointing. A billboard pronounced Bandera as the cowboy capital of the world.

"Who knew cowboys had a capital," she said, captivated by the idea of it.

The odors of coffee and cinnamon lured them to the door of a stucco shop. A weathered canopy covered an outdoor seating area.

"Shall we sit outside?" Tyler asked.

"Better yet, let's get the drinks to go," she said. "Walking helps me unwind and the town is so interesting."

"Suits me. I've never liked sitting in one place too long. Gives the enemy an easy target."

The careless comment caused a knot to form in Julie's throat. The talk of danger had been all about her, but Tyler lived with it every day when he was on active duty.

"How much longer until your tour of duty is over?" she asked, hating to even think he'd go back to a war so far from home.

"It all depends on whether or not I reenlist."

"And what does that depend on?"

"What kind of coffee do you want?" he asked, changing the subject.

"An iced caramel latte," she said. "With whipped cream."

Tyler's brows arched. "Are we celebrating something?"

"Spring. Bluebonnets. Cowboys. And serendipity."

As expected, Tyler had no response to that, either.

When they returned to the street, fresh brew in hand, the wind had picked up and a few fluffy clouds had drifted in. The town was no less intriguing with her hair being whipped about her face.

"Arkey Blue's Silver Dollar Saloon, established in the 1930s, or so says the sign." She stopped to take a second look. "Do you realize how many decades that is?"

"Long enough for the place to have seen its share of good times."

"There are a lot of honky-tonks on this one street," she said.

"Cowboys are known to play as hard as they work."

"I like that about them," Julie said. "Actually, you're the first real cowboy I've ever met, at least since I've been an adult," she admitted. "There weren't a lot of genuine cowboys in New Orleans."

He grinned and tossed his empty cup into a green waste can. "Too bad I'm just a fake."

"Yeah, well, I was sure wrong about that. You're for real even if those boots are new."

"What makes you think so?"

"I've seen you with Dylan and Sean and your dad. You're all real cowboys, tough but gentle. Protective. Self-reliant. The kind of man you can trust and believe in."

"Troy was convicted of murder. That doesn't exactly make him a hero in my book." The bitterness slipped into his voice. "And for the record, Julie, I'm no hero, either. So don't go reading those things into me."

She'd said too much. Tyler continued to walk at her side, but he'd pulled away in every way that mattered. But she was right about him. He was the real thing. He just hadn't found his way all the way home yet.

An hour later, they parked in front of Janie's Shears. Once again the sign on the door said Closed. Disappointment curdled in Julie's stomach.

"I guess the trip to Mustang Run was a waste of time," she said. "But Abby assured me yesterday that Janie would be working today."

"Something must have come up to keep her from opening the shop."

"Which means I have to wait another day to see if she has a relative named Zeke."

"What's plan B?" Tyler asked.

"Locate and follow the paper trail. That would be easier if I had any idea what part of the country he's living in now."

"I'd suggest you start with Texas," Tyler said. "If he's from around here, chances are he didn't travel too far away."

"And yet you may reenlist to go back to the Middle East."

He gave her a quizzical look as if he had no idea why she'd brought that up again.

She hated that she had, but she couldn't get his leaving off her mind. One kiss, and her head was full of Tyler. This at a time when all her thoughts should be on the Frost case. And on staying alive.

"How about a burger at Abby's since we're right here?" Tyler asked. "It's only a quarter to twelve. We can beat the downtown lunch bunch."

"She'll think her pie lured me back and be pleased," Julie said.

"She'll be surprised to see you with me. And don't get paranoid if people get up and walk out when I walk in."

"Why would they?"

"I'm a son of Troy Ledger. Everybody doesn't forgive and forget."

Including Tyler.

"The last time you were here, you were only eight years old. No one will recognize you."

"You've seen one Ledger, you've seen them all," he quipped.

That wasn't exactly true, but there was a distinct resemblance between him and Sean and Dylan. And all three of them knock-dead hunks. But there were distinct differences, as well.

Nonetheless, to her surprise, there were some raised eyebrows when they entered together. A couple frowns of disapproval. Fewer welcoming smiles than she'd received yesterday. Fewer nods. Only one hello and that was from the same elderly man she'd run into yesterday. The gray-haired woman with the walker didn't look up from the plastic menu she was studying.

The waitress, however, was all smiles, her appreciation for good-looking cowboys as obvious as yesterday.

"You're back," she said to Julie, though her smile appeared to be all for Tyler. "Abby said you would be."

"That Abby must be a fortune teller."

"Nope. It's the pies. Some people drive clear from Austin and then buy two or three whole ones to take home with them."

"Then I'll have to have pie," Tyler said. "But I'll start with the jalapeño Angus burger, the half-pounder, with a side of onion rings and a tall glass of iced tea."

"Sweet or unsweetened?" She leaned extra close using the excuse of straightening the artificial sweetener crib as she talked.

"Sweetened, of course."

"You sound like a man with a hearty appetite. And you look like a bull rider with all those muscles."

"Just the appetite. No bull."

She laughed as if that were the funniest comment she'd heard in weeks. Julie realized with a shock that she was jealous. She and Tyler were not a couple. Yet, sitting here watching the waitress flirt so openly, she had to admit that she was much hungrier for another of his kisses than she was for anything on Abby's menu—including pie.

UNDER NORMAL CIRCUMSTANCES, Tyler could have finished off the oversize burger and the plate of crispy onion rings and had room for half of one of Abby's famous pies. Today he had trouble getting the burger and rings down. His mind was on what he and Julie had left mostly unspoken this morning—the crime scene photo missing from the file.

The real-deal killer might well be the person determined to stop Julie from pulling the old case out of the freezer. Was he afraid she'd uncover new evidence to tie him to the crime or had it always been there, overlooked by Grayson as a young, inexperienced deputy?

DNA. Motive. A fake alibi.

Julie had ignored his threats. Now he might be ready to make good on them. Tyler was here to see that the threats weren't carried out. But he was only here for a little more than a week.

Tyler turned to watch her eat. She had the fork in her hand, but she was merely moving the shrimp salad around on her plate.

"Is the food okay?"

She put down the fork. "It's good. I'm just not hungry. Too much on my mind."

He reached for her hand and squeezed it. A spiral of raw need flamed inside him, and he wondered again how someone he had just met could have such a profound impact on his libido. It could be the danger, but it seemed like a whole lot more than just physical attraction.

Sitting here in the midst of all these strangers, he ached to feel her lips on his again.

A smiling middle-aged woman with a flour-smeared apron sidled up to their booth. "Ah, I see you did come back and you brought a friend."

"I did," Julie said. "I told him that you'd cornered the market on flaky and delicious."

"Now you see why I sometimes give away pie."

"It was delicious, but actually I came into town to talk to Janie Hartwell. I was upset to see that her shop is closed again today."

"And I hate to tell you, but it will be for two more days. Emma Sue from the drug store was just in and she said Janie's daughter went into labor early. Janie shut down the shop so she could rush over to Houston and be on hand for the birth of her first grandchild. I haven't heard if she made it on time or not."

So there went that option. Frustration killed Julie's smile.

"Sorry," Abby said. "You might check around town. Somebody will know if Tom has a brother named Zeke. Or else they'll be able to give you Janie's cell phone number."

"Thanks." Julie turned back to Tyler as if just remembering he were there. "Tyler, this is Abby. She owns the diner."

"Tyler." She narrowed her eyes. "Tyler Ledger." Abby's hands flew to the top of her head and her eyes got big as saucers. "I can't believe I didn't recognize you the second I saw you."

"I've changed since age eight."

"Yes, but you look just like your father did at your age. Troy moved into the area and had every female from fourteen to forty swooning over him."

"Not a lot of swooning going on in here," Tyler said.

"I can't believe no one told me that you were in town."

"I surprised the family, and I'm only here for a few more days."

"Three sons back in Texas all at once. I bet Troy has to chisel the grin off his face every morning before he can shave."

Tyler let the comment ride.

The bell over the front door tinkled and a tall lawman in a khaki uniform and a worn brown Stetson stepped through the door. The guy was a bit stooped through the shoulders, but an authoritative air clung to him like cheap aftershave as he swaggered into the diner.

Abby got his attention and waved him back to their booth. "That's Glenn McGuire, our sheriff."

The sheriff spoke to half the customers on his way back. When he finally reached them, he put his arm around Abby's shoulder. "Shouldn't you be in the kitchen baking?"

She smiled and swayed her hips into his. "I get breaks. Bet you can't guess who this is," she said, pointing at Tyler.

"Tyler Ledger," the sheriff said. It was clear he wasn't guessing.

Without waiting for an invitation that wasn't going to come, Sheriff McGuire slid into the booth opposite them.

"I've got the chicken fried steak on special," Abby said.

McGuire waved off the suggestion. "Ham and cheese sandwich on rye, easy on the mustard, and a cup of coffee. No fries."

Abby leaned an elbow on the back of McGuire's gray plastic seat. "My, but you're getting persnickety in your old age."

"It's the festival doings. All these strangers piling into town are giving me ulcers."

"Ham sandwich coming up. And what kind of pie can I get you, Tyler? On the house, the least I can do for a serviceman."

"I can't possibly swallow another bite."

"Then I'll get you one to take home."

"Buttermilk pie?" Julie asked, her tone teasing.

Abby gave her a wink. "Buttermilk."

Tyler had no idea what that was about.

Julie introduced herself to Sheriff McGuire as Abby walked away.

"I know who you are and why you're in Mustang Run," he said. "Collette told me. You're wasting your time if you think you're going to tie Helene Ledger's murder to Muriel Frost's."

Collette had obviously not inherited her bubbly personality from her dad.

"What makes you so sure I'm wasting my time?" Julie asked.

"I investigated Helene's murder and I did a dadburn good job of it, no matter what Troy thinks. I didn't find any evidence that the two were related."

Tyler looked the sheriff straight in the eye. "So you took all the circumstantial evidence and decided my father was guilty."

"I was the officer in charge, not the judge and jury, so don't go trying to place blame on me."

"I'm just after the facts," Tyler assured him. "Did you run across the name Zeke Hartwell in your investigation?"

"As a matter of fact, I did. He was a suspect in the Frost murder for awhile, as well, but he was cleared."

"Cleared based on an alibi that may have been flawed," Julie said.

"I don't know anything about that. That case wasn't in my jurisdiction, but I've got no reason to think the investigation wasn't handled well. I know for certain Zeke Hartwell wasn't responsible for Helene's murder."

"Because of an ironclad alibi?" Tyler asked.

"As ironclad as you can get. He was in the Lubbock jail at the time for putting his seven-months'-pregnant wife in the hospital. Knocked out some of her teeth and broke a couple ribs, if I remember correctly. And he kicked his wife in the stomach. The wife survived. The baby didn't."

McGuire did have a way of cutting right to the nitty-gritty. Tyler had to admit he liked that about the man.

McGuire propped his elbows on the narrow table. "You don't want to tangle with Zeke Hartwell, Julie. He's buck-snorting mean. I wouldn't put anything past the guy."

"I'll keep that in mind," she promised.

Abby returned with the pie in a white to-go box. "Your order will be right out, Sheriff. And Tyler, it's real nice having you back in town. And tell that father of yours I expect to see him at the dance on Thursday night. People might gawk and talk at first, but they'll get past it."

Tyler wasn't so sure about that. He drove by the park as they were leaving town. Small tents were being set up around the perimeter. A large tent was going up near the gazebo, no doubt for the dance Abby had mentioned. Tyler stopped at a red light behind a pickup truck loaded with folding tables.

He reached across the space between them and rested

his hand on Julie's shoulder. "I'm thinking we should go to the dance."

She looked surprised. "Any particular reason?"

"So that I have a good excuse to hold you in my arms."

Julie leaned in close. "You don't need an excuse for that."

She pressed her lips against his. Desire hit with so much force that he had to keep one hand on the wheel to stay grounded. Her breath mingled with his, and the taste of her was like liquid fire shooting through his veins.

The honk of a car horn finally yanked him back to reality.

"To be continued," he said.

"At the dance." She smiled and traced her lips with the tip of her tongue, all but driving him mad.

He was going to make love with Julie. They were moving toward that at rocket speed.

And then what? The answer was a no-brainer. And then he'd go back to the battlefield with memories of Julie burning in his mind. Romance was the last thing he'd expected to find in Mustang Run. And the last thing he needed, when it had no chance to last.

Still he didn't think he could wait to hold her in his arms, on or off the dance floor.

A lemon yellow Jaguar convertible was parked in front of the house when they returned to Willow Creek Ranch. "More company," Julie noted. "I predict another homemade casserole for dinner tonight."

Troy met them on the porch. "There's a Candice

Cameron here to see you, Julie. She says it has to do with your investigation."

Tyler had a disturbing hunch that this would not be good.

CANDICE APPEARED TO BE IN her mid-fifties, though from the thick layers of makeup she wore, age was difficult to judge. Her ears dripped with dangling diamonds and silver balls in some kind of chunky, contemporary design. Her fingers flashed diamonds and rubies. Her straight black skirt was chic, the red silk blouse provocative.

Troy and Tyler had disappeared quickly, leaving Julie to entertain her surprise guest in the family area.

"Can I get you something?" Julie asked. "Water? Coffee? A soda?"

"No, thanks. I don't have much time, since I've already been waiting for over an hour."

"We didn't have an appointment," Julie reminded her.

"I realize that," Candice said, "but Sheriff Grayson told me that you were staying with Troy Ledger and I really wanted the chance to talk to you. I was afraid you might not see me if I called first."

"Why wouldn't I?" Julie asked.

"I didn't know what the sheriff might have told you about me."

"He said you were off-limits, but there's no law that I know of against talking to whomever I choose."

"I'm glad you feel that way. Sheriff Grayson doesn't like you interfering in this, but I don't understand why.

You'd think he'd want all the help he could get seeing as how he never found Muriel's killer."

"Already we agree on something," Julie said. "I'm glad you came."

"So am I. Muriel didn't just work for us, she and I were really good friends. I wasn't sure if anyone had told you that."

"Kara Saunders mentioned that to me."

"You've talked to Kara?"

"I did, just a few days ago, in fact."

"Kara was a trip and a half. I still miss her, but she was never as crazy after Muriel was killed. I'm talking about the good kind of crazy. The kind that makes you laugh. Kara, Muriel and I had some really good times together. I guess Kara told you about that."

"We didn't get to talk much."

"Anyway, if you're doing a story about Muriel's murder, I thought you should hear some of the good things about her."

"Why don't you tell me some of those?" Julie took out the notebook and pen she'd been using in the car.

"Sure. Muriel was smart and pretty. Petite, but not so little that she didn't have curves in all the right places. And she had this flirty way about her that drew the attention of every man she met. We all joked that you should lock up your husband when Muriel came around."

"She must have inspired a lot of jealousy."

"Too much and most of it unfounded. When women took the time to know Muriel, they found she had a heart of gold and didn't want *their* husbands. That's the Muriel I knew."

"You don't think she was killed by a jealous wife?"

"No. I think she got involved with the wrong people."

"What wrong people?"

"Able Drake for one. He was exciting, but trouble. He always had a beautiful woman on his arm. Troy Ledger can tell you about him. They were friends back then. My guess is that they still are, though Able is a respected Dallas socialite now."

"What was he back then?"

"The U.S. connection for a Mexican drug cartel. Drug running is not new, you know. It's been going on for years. It's just getting a lot of media coverage now. But that's how Able Drake made all his money. And believe me, he has plenty."

"Were they still together when she was murdered?"

"No. Able was furious when she agreed to raise her niece, even ordered her not to. When she took the girl anyway, he walked out on her."

Julie's chest tightened. "So she gave up a lot to take in her sister's child?"

"A lot of trash if you ask me. I never cared for Able. I'm sure you know how her niece came to live with her."

"Why don't you tell me?"

Julie shifted nervously and wondered if anything Candice was telling her was the truth or if she had reasons for concocting her own version of history.

"Muriel's sister was killed in a brawl up in some Tulsa roadhouse where she was working as a barmaid. She was a good woman and a good mother, but then her husband deserted her and she got hooked on street drugs. It broke Muriel's heart to see her niece so neglected."

"How do you know this?"

"Muriel confided in me when her sister was killed. Muriel flew right up to Oklahoma and got the little girl. I lent her the money for the plane ticket. It was less than two hundred dollars, but Muriel didn't have it. She paid me back, though, wrote me a check right before she died."

A check for $186. That explained that check. And if Candice was telling the truth about that, then everything she said might be accurate.

"Her niece was a scared, pitiful creature. She'd hardly even talked to Muriel when she first arrived. And then she lost her mother and her aunt in a matter of months. I doubt that little girl ever recovered from that."

"I wouldn't count the niece out," Julie said, fighting her own reaction to a few details she was hearing for the first time. "Some people are a lot more resilient than you'd ever imagine."

Julie was reeling from all the new information. Candice seemed genuine, but she couldn't be sure.

Candice scooted her chair closer and cupped her mouth. "Muriel isn't the only reason I came here today."

Now they just might be getting somewhere.

"I don't think it's safe for you to stay in this house," she whispered. "I don't know what happened to Helene Ledger, but I'm convinced that Able Drake had something to do with Muriel's murder, probably because she knew too much about his business. I wouldn't trust him or Troy, especially if you start getting too close to the truth."

Suspicions clattered in Julie's mind like a summer hailstorm. Able Drake had been questioned by Grayson. She'd seen a report of that in the file though there was no mention that he was involved in drugs or of his relationship with Troy Ledger. But then he'd been questioned months before Helene's murder.

What if Drake had also killed Helene? If it was true that he liked beautiful women, he might have lured Helene into an affair, as well. Or Troy might have caught them together and gone into a rage.

What would Tyler say if she did discover that his father was guilty of killing Helene? Was it even ethical for her to be staying in this house, knowing what she did about Able Drake?

Only she wasn't sure that any of what she'd heard was factual. Candice Cameron might have orchestrated the interview to lay blame on Able.

Julie was thankful a few minutes later when Candice said she had to go. Julie needed time alone to think. She flew off the porch and started walking as Candice drove away. She didn't realize she headed directly toward the horse barn until she heard the beckoning of a whinny.

Guinevere would have her hands full if she was supposed to give Julie perspective now.

WHATEVER CANDICE CAMERON HAD come to say had apparently not sat well with Julie. Tyler watched from the back steps as she stormed away from the house on foot, not even slowing as she stamped through a thick patch of bluebonnets.

Had she wanted him, she'd have come looking for him instead of forging out on her own, he told himself. She may look like a youthful burst of energy and feel like innocent vulnerability in his arms, but she was competent and determined, a force to be reckoned with.

He gave her a half hour to herself and then started walking in the same direction she had, through the sun-drenched bluebonnets and along the trail to the horse barn. He stepped from the heat of the sun into the shade and shadows of the barn. When his eyes adjusted to the change in light, he spotted Julie, curled up practically in a ball just outside Guinevere's stall.

"I thought I might find you here."

"I needed a place to think."

"About whatever the rich witch of cosmetic land had to say?"

"About how the facts in the case keep twisting into new coils, each one more bizarre than the last."

"Do you want to talk about it?"

She stood and stuffed her hands into the pockets of her jeans, her perky breasts poking out from her ramrod stance.

"No. I want to forget about it for one whole hour. I want to think of absolutely nothing except sunshine and wildflowers and…. And you, Tyler. I want to go somewhere and concentrate on you. The only unknown in my life who isn't involved in a murder mystery."

"I'm game as long as you're not thinking of playing twenty questions."

"What's wrong with that? I used to love that game."

"I don't know twenty answers."

"I'm quite sure you underestimate yourself."

"How about a horseback ride?" he asked. "Nothing like the wind in your face and the feel of a good horse beneath you to provide the perfect escape."

Julie glanced around her. "I told you that I'm not quite ready for that."

"That was then. This is now. You could ride Lady. Collette says she's extra gentle."

"Which one is Lady?"

"The mare right behind you."

Julie looked at the horse and frowned. "You want me to climb up there? I'd need a stepladder."

"You'd only need me." His voice grew husky.

Julie took a deep breath and exhaled slowly. "How about we take a ride in your truck and save Lady for next time?"

"If that's what you want."

"It is. Can I hear a *Yee-haw?*"

She was joking again, but frustration still colored her voice.

In minutes, they were in Tyler's truck and bumping and shimmying along rough ranch roads. Without thinking about it, he ended up at the swimming hole.

Memories rushed into his consciousness, this time all good ones. He could practically hear the laughter and yells of his brothers as they swung out over the pool.

Amazingly the old rope was still there, the gnarled strings coming unwound.

"What a beautiful spot," Julie said. "We should have

packed a picnic, not that I'm hungry." She jumped out of the car and started walking toward the water.

Tyler set the emergency brake and joined her.

"The water is crystal clear," she proclaimed. She reached down, made of cup of her hand and splashed the water on her face. "And cold."

"It's always cold, even in the summer. It's spring fed."

"A spring-fed pool for a swimming hole. Now that's living."

It had been when he was a kid.

Julie kicked out of her shoes and rolled up her jeans. She stuck one toe in and twirled it about in the water. "That first dip is a shock to the system, but it's refreshing once you get used to it."

She walked back to where he was standing. "How old are you, Tyler?"

"Twenty-six. You?"

"Twenty-five. How is it you're not in a serious relationship?"

"Not a lot of opportunity when you're fighting a war."

"But before that. Were you ever engaged?"

He leaned against the rough trunk of a pine tree. "Your twenty questions are about up. Are you sure you want to waste one of them on that?"

She scooted close and put her arms around his neck. "Why do you always change the subject instead of talking about yourself?"

"I hate to be bored."

"Oh, no. You're not going to wisecrack out of this one. Why do you keep me at a distance?"

"I never had a lot of practice in opening up."

"You could learn. You'll never know unless you give it a try." Julie pulled away. "Do you know a man named Able Drake?"

"Not if he's a shrink you're about to recommend."

"He's not, but I think he could be a friend of your father's."

"Now that you mention it, that name did come up the other day."

"What did he say about him?"

"That he is the kind of friend who he can count on in a crunch. Why do you ask?"

"Candice said Muriel was romantically involved with him."

"Troy never mentioned that. What else did Candice say?"

"Nothing much. She just wanted me to know that she and Muriel were good friends. One more question. Why is it you never call your father *Dad?*"

"Are you sure you're not a trial attorney?"

"That's not a hard question, Tyler. Just the simple truth would work."

There was no simple truth. "I had a dad once, a long time ago. The body may be the same, except older. But the man inside the body that goes by the name of Troy Ledger isn't that man."

"Give him a chance. He might be again."

"Or I could find out that he never was the man I believed him to be. Now let's talk about you."

"I'm an only child, spoiled rotten, didn't take advantage of the educational opportunities offered to me, so I ended up telling teenage girls how to dress, what not to text and how to say no to the hot guy in your senior class who wants to steal your virginity.

"And one day I'm going to be a high-profile investigative reporter who major news networks jockey for the privilege of paying the big bucks. And I'll make a difference in the world."

"Unless you get killed on your first case."

"Well, there's that. And I'm tired of talking about it, so I'm going to strip out of my clothes and go dive into that inviting, spring-fed pool."

She reached under the hem of her blouse, caught hold of it and yanked it over her head. As if that wasn't bad enough, she gave her seductive hips an extra swing or two as she twirled the shirt over her head and tossed it to the ground.

She looked back at him. "Coming?"

Without waiting for an answer, she continued stripping her way to the water. The bra was the next to go. Wiggling out of the jeans took a bit more time. And then she was down to the skimpiest pair of red bikini panties he'd ever seen.

She slipped a thumb under the waistband and stood in one spot while she peeled the scrap of silky fabric from her body.

Tyler's sexual energy topped the charts. The desire to pull Julie's naked body against his felt like an explosion ripping through his body.

None of the reasons he'd come up with earlier for keeping her at a distance reached his passion-muddled brain.

Tyler shed his clothes in record time and plunged into the icy water, so overcome with his need for Julie that he never even felt the cold.

Chapter Eight

The plunge stole Julie's breath. She closed her eyes and swam beneath the surface of the shallow water, smooth, steady strokes to warm her. The exercise felt good, but it didn't begin to soothe the frustrations that haunted her.

Able Drake. His connection with Troy Ledger. The fear that Troy might not be totally innocent.

The way she hungered for Tyler.

She felt a gentle tug on her leg which caused her to stop, plant her feet. When she opened her eyes, now above water, Tyler pulled her into his arms. The frustrations dissolved into honeyed gold as the thrill of Tyler filled her.

A heated slickness slid between them as he cuddled her in his arms. He was standing on bottom and she pulled up her legs and wrapped them around his hips.

He kissed her then, a slow, wet, consuming kiss that shook her senses and left her trembling. "You really know how to push a man over the edge, Julie Gillespie."

His kisses grew more ravenous and she kissed him

back just as madly, twice as deliciously. She loved her body locked with his with nothing but the glaze of moisture to separate them. She loved the feel of her hands splayed across the smooth, muscular flesh of his back. Loved the hard push of his erection against her naked flesh.

"You're the best part of Texas," Tyler whispered. "You're the one thing worth coming home for." He trailed kisses down her neck and nuzzled his mouth in the hollow formed by the gentle swell of her cleavage.

Lowering his head, he nibbled her right nipple, creating heated sensations that swept through her like a fever. And then his hand slid between her legs, finding the sweet spot that turned her core to liquid gold.

He played her one finger a time, pressing, kneading, titillating until her wetness was like a bubble of heat at his fingertips.

"I'm not sure…" His voice got caught on emotion.

Julie shushed him with her mouth on his. "Don't try to explain this, Tyler. You want me. I want you. Just let that be enough."

"It's so much more than enough. What about protection?"

"Oh, cripes, Tyler. What a time to think of that."

"Are you on the pill?"

"Yes, but only because of some hormonal problems. I haven't been with a man in forever. But I have had a physical lately."

"Same here. The army has taken care of both of late. Kept me so busy fighting, there's no time or opportunity for sex. Checked me for everything contagious known to man."

"I love the army." Julie slid down his body, letting her belly ride the length of him before she cradled the tip of his erection in her hands. All that pulsing, burning need throbbing in her hand was for her. Her head began to spin. She was crazed with the ecstasy, hungry for all of him.

"Don't wait, Tyler. Make love with me here in the water. Not for yesterday or tomorrow, but for now. For us."

"Oh, Julie, how could I ever turn that down?"

He lifted her again and then lowered her onto his throbbing shaft. She felt him inside her, hot and wet and needing her the way she needed him.

His breathing came in short, quick gasps. His chest heaved and his pulsing rhythm rocked her until her body trembled with the intensity of her climax.

He held her until they both were spent. Then he relaxed his arms and let her ride down his weakened body to the rocky bottom of the pool.

She flipped to her back and floated away from him and into a thousand fanciful dreams that would never come true. But today was real. The memories would live inside her forever, a buffer for the heartbreak to come when Tyler left her for good.

SLEEP REFUSED TO COME THAT night and Julie lay awake until well past midnight, tossing in the guest room bed and thinking how nice it would be to go knock on Tyler's door and crawl into bed with him. She imagined his body curled around hers. He'd kiss the area between her shoulder blades while he caressed her breasts.

She'd snuggle all the closer, and even their toes would kiss between the cool sheets.

Only Tyler had shown no sign of wanting her in his bed. Making love with him had been perfect. She had no doubt that it had been as electrifying for him as it had been for her.

But when they'd come back to the house, Dylan and Sean had been waiting. The three brothers had stayed on the porch and talked until almost dark.

Julie had gone out once to offer them a beer and caught enough of the conversation to know that the discussion was about the future and whether or not Tyler would return to the ranch when he finished his current tour of duty.

After Dylan and Sean had left, Tyler had withdrawn into himself. The kitchen had been thick with tension at supper and even before she and Troy had finished their soup and salads, Tyler had excused himself saying he wanted to catch the weather report on the local TV channel.

The only hint that he even remembered the lovemaking they'd shared had been the secretive and almost casual kiss he'd given her when he'd said good-night.

If her heart felt as if it were starting to shatter, she had no one to blame but herself. She knew from the start this relationship had nowhere to go. She just hadn't expected it to deteriorate so fast.

But at least Tyler had been honest with her. He

was here for another week. He never suggested their relationship would last longer than that.

Julie, on the other hand, had been dishonest from the beginning. She'd lied to Tyler or at least omitted a few basic truths. She'd lied to Troy. It was possible she'd even lied to herself about who she was and why she was so driven to find Muriel's killer.

At ten minutes before two a.m., Julie gave up on falling asleep. She climbed out of bed and padded barefoot to the sliding glass door. Pushing back the opaque curtain, she peered into the garden.

Moonlight shimmered and danced in the spraying fountain near the antique bench, inviting, yet slightly eerie. Julie eased the door open but couldn't totally avoid the squeak of the metal sliding across metal.

"Are you having trouble sleeping, too?"

She jumped at the voice, her heart slamming against her chest.

Troy stepped from behind a large pot of wisteria.

"I didn't realize you were out here," she said.

"It's where I come when I can't sleep. Helene created this garden. It was her refuge from the shenanigans of the five rambunctious boys who filled the house."

"I can see why. It's so peaceful."

"I know it sounds strange," Troy said, "but when I'm here all alone, I sometimes feel her presence so strongly that I talk to her out loud."

Troy stepped to the bench and wrapped his fingers around the back of it as if it might dissolve into the night if he didn't hold it down.

"Do you want to talk about Helene?"

Troy didn't answer. He just stood there, gripping the back of the bench and staring across the garden as if he were waiting for his dead wife to join him.

"I loved her from the day I first laid eyes on her," Troy said. "She was Glenn McGuire's girlfriend, but when he brought her home from college for the weekend, I didn't care that Glenn was my best friend. All I knew was that I had to find a way to make Helene mine."

"She must have fallen for you, as well."

"Yes, that was the beauty of it. We both felt it at the same time. We both knew we were meant to be together."

"You were very lucky."

He nodded. "And even luckier when the boys came along. I know Helene wanted a girl, but she never showed one glimmer of disappointment. She was as excited with Dakota as she was with Wyatt."

"It's too bad her parents never accepted the marriage."

"It is. Helene tried to tell them that what we shared was a million times more satisfying than the things their money could buy. Her words fell on deaf ears. All they could see was that she didn't have the kind of luxurious lifestyle they could have provided her."

Julie felt his anguish, but still she couldn't turn off her reporter mind-set with its invasive curiosity. "They say you never really fought to prove your innocence during the trial. Why was that?"

Troy worried the jagged scar that punctuated the right side of his face. "I died inside when I discovered Helene's bloodied body." His voice lowered as if the loss still had the power to suck away his strength.

"I went to a place so dark, I couldn't find my way. I let Helene down when she needed me most to be strong for our sons. I will never forgive myself for that. But I can't undo the past. I just have to go on as best I can."

Any doubts that Julie had about Troy's innocence faded into oblivion. It was as if the pain in his voice erupted from his soul. No one could fake the kind of raw, heartrending emotion she was witnessing now.

"All your sons will forgive you in time."

"Perhaps. Tyler doesn't seem so inclined. I reach out to him, but there's no forgiveness there. He's closed off, cold somewhere deep inside."

"He's bitter about the past," Julie admitted. "But he's not cold inside." Anything but. He'd proven that when they'd made love. "He keeps too much walled off inside him, but that doesn't mean he won't come around in time. He wouldn't have come home at all if he wasn't seeking something from you and his brothers."

"That's what Eve told me on the phone this afternoon. I hope you're both right."

"I hope so, too, for both your sakes."

Troy smiled and raked his fingers through his slightly graying hair. "You should have seen Tyler as a kid. He was the most outgoing of all. He jumped into life like it was a roller-coaster ride and he didn't want to miss a single thrill."

The way he'd jumped into their lovemaking today.

But then he'd drawn back inside himself. Tough

as nails. Afraid of nothing except letting down his emotional guard.

Julie knew that and still she couldn't keep from falling for him.

"The one thing I can do for Helene and my sons is to find her killer," Troy said. "I can't give our sons back their childhood, but I will avenge their mother's murder. I won't rest until I've done that, not if it takes me the rest of my life."

Julie walked over and stood next to him, letting her fingers link with his on the cold hard metal. "I believe you, Troy. You must have loved Helene very, very much."

Troy pulled away and dabbed at the moisture in his eye with the back of his sleeve. "I still love her. That's the thing about true love. Your life may change in a million ways. You may even lose that person to death. But that love remains forever."

Days ago Julie might have argued that fact. But that was before she met Tyler, before they'd made love. For the first time in her life, she could see how love might last forever.

Julie lingered in the garden even after Troy had said good-night and returned to his room. Even then Helene's presence felt as real as the scent of jasmine and as moving as the gentle breeze.

JULIE SPENT MOST OF THURSDAY shut up in the guest room or sequestered in the courtyard garden trying to merge Troy's notes, her notes and the police file. It was more confusing than trying to solve a crossword puzzle in a foreign language.

It didn't help that since making love to Tyler, he was perpetually on her mind. It only made it worse that she'd barely seen him since then and they'd had no time alone. She wasn't even certain that he still planned to take her to the festival dance tonight.

Sean and Dylan had kept him busy with activities around the ranch all day. Julie had intentionally stayed out of the way as much as she could. After all, she was the intruder here—and she had work to do. Mostly, she didn't want Tyler or his brothers to see how she reacted to even the slightest touch or smidgen of attention from Tyler.

She ached to feel his arms around her again, was dying to taste his kisses. She'd fantasized making love to him in every picturesque spot on this scenic ranch.

But the next move would be up to him.

Julie stretched and struggled to get her thoughts back on target. Now that she'd completely ruled out Troy as Helene's killer, the serial killer theory seemed even more plausible. The murders could have been random with no previous connection between the perpetrator and the victim. She'd researched and talked to enough cops to know those were the hardest cases to solve, especially when the killer left no distinct signature.

Julie had spent almost an hour on the phone this morning with her trusted police contact, Mac Rainer, in New Orleans. Mac also voiced the opinion that pictures of the victims could be a madman's souvenir of his crime.

He warned her of the danger she was facing if the picture and threat left on her windshield had been left there by a serial killer.

But if the acts of violence were random, that would also rule out Zeke Hartwell and Able Drake as suspects. Julie wasn't ready to go with either of those exclusions yet.

So she'd had done a little tracking on her own, using tactics she'd picked up while working at the newspaper and from private investigation source books.

The last permanent address she could find on Zeke was in Abilene, Texas, and that had been over a year ago. Troy had that information in his records.

Able Drake had been easy to track down. He owned a huge and prosperous ranch south of Dallas. He'd become one of those Texas legends: bad boy turned rich, turned good and now was one of the wealthiest men in Texas. Even Guy Cameron's portfolio paled in comparison.

Muriel would have met Able during the bad-boy stage when he might have been capable of any atrocity. But Able wasn't responsible for the picture left on Julie's car, not unless he'd paid someone to do it for him. He was out of the country, spending a few months on his yacht sailing around Greece.

The police files were practically useless. There was a dearth of information. There had never been a firm suspect and no arrests were ever made in the Frost case.

According to a report written by Caleb Grayson, the cause of death had been the shots fired into Muriel's head. But the medical examiner's report itself was missing from the file.

Julie had put in a call to Sheriff Grayson to ask about that omission, but he hadn't returned her call. She doubted that he would, which meant if she wanted the ME report, she'd have to track the sheriff down or see if the office of the ME would release the information directly to her.

Dropping the folder to the desk, she opened the top drawer and took out the picture of Muriel in her red broomstick skirt and white peasant blouse. She looked positively regal with her hair piled into an upsweep. And the long, red skirt fit her slim hips to perfection.

Julie set the picture on the desk and pulled the ponytail holder from her hair, letting her blond locks fall free. She bent over, shook out her hair and then gathered it into a loose ball on top of her head.

The reflection smiling back at her looked amazingly like the image in the photo.

But who was the suitor in the picture with Muriel? Who had she ripped from the photo and why?

And could he somehow be the man behind her murder?

Julie held the skirt to her waist and waltzed about the room as murder and conspiracy theories danced in her head.

All of a sudden she knew why she'd bought that peasant blouse and what she'd wear to the dance tonight. And she would attend the event even if she had to do so alone.

She would go as Muriel Frost.

Julie stripped out of her clothes and stepped into the

shower. She'd have to start the transformation now if she was going to be ready in time for the dance.

She stood beneath the spray as the rivulets of water careened into all the sensual crevices where Tyler's fingers had touched her. She ran her hand down her belly and let it slide between her own legs. Her body vibrated with a crazed need for Tyler to make love with her again.

Memories might be all she was left with when Tyler returned to active duty, but she craved more than memories now.

DYLAN HANDED OUT COLD bottles of beer all around. Tyler took one and leaned against the front porch banister, trying to concentrate on what Dylan was saying.

While Dylan and Sean were talking ranching, Tyler was thinking about Julie and how to keep her safe.

The most obvious solution was the easiest. She could drop the Frost investigation. There were thousands of cold cases out there that wouldn't put her life in danger. No doubt, some were even more fascinating than the Frost case. In fact, the most interesting thing it had going for it was the unfortunate niece who witnessed the atrocious crime.

"You can see there's plenty of room for you in the ranching business," Dylan said. "If we buy the McGillis property and add it to what we've already got, we can maintain impressive herds of longhorns and Angus. And I've talked to McGillis. He's willing to deal."

The pressure started building between Tyler's temples. "I don't know that I'm ready for this."

"Is it the Hill Country you don't want to return to or ranching?" Dylan asked, clearly puzzled that Tyler wasn't jumping at the chance to move back home and go into business with him.

"Or is it Dad?" Sean asked.

No use not to level with his brothers. Tyler took a long swig of beer and tried to pull his thoughts together. "I'm not as sure of Troy's innocence as you guys seem to be."

"Dad's obsessed with finding Mom's killer," Sean said. "What other proof do you need?"

"All my life I was told he had murdered Mother. By Aunt Sibley, Grandma, Grandpa. I had no reason to doubt them. And Troy was convicted by a jury."

"I was right there where you are at one time," Dylan admitted. "But when you get to know Dad, you know he couldn't have done it. Collette was convinced of his innocence even before I was."

"I'm sorry, guys. I just don't see myself fitting into this whole united-family scheme of things."

"There's nothing to be sorry for," Sean said. "You have every right to live your life the way you want, even if that means reenlisting. Some people are meant to be soldiers. I'd hate to think what shape the world would be in now if we didn't have brave warriors."

"It's not even that," Tyler said. "I'm not sure I want to stay in the army. And I like the ranching life. I like the wide-open spaces, like seeing the new calves and colts come into the world. I'd love to be here to help with roundup and to go to auction."

The words spilled out now that he'd started leveling

with them. He could learn to love it here if things were different between him and Troy. "I'm just not ready to commit to coming home for good."

"Maybe you're just too worried about Julie to deal with all of this," Dylan said.

Tyler watched his expression to see if there was any malice in the statement. He saw none.

"I said things when she first arrived I shouldn't have," Dylan said. "I can see how you feel about her and I know you're determined to keep her safe. I get it. I felt that same way about Collette, not too many months ago."

"Why don't you give Wyatt a call," Sean suggested. "What's the use of having a big brother who's an infamous Atlanta homicide detective if you can't yell for help when you need to?"

"Good point," Dylan said. "I can't believe we haven't thought of that sooner."

"Because we were too busy trying to find a way to get Tyler back to the ranch," Sean said. "I've got Wyatt's number in my phone. I'll ring him for you."

"I'm not sure how he'll help," Tyler said.

"Just lay the facts on the line. He has an uncanny ability to see the big picture in police matters."

Wyatt's phone was ringing when Sean passed his cell phone to Tyler.

"Hit me."

"Wyatt."

"Yeah?"

"It's me, Tyler." No response. "Tyler Ledger. Your brother."

"Well, it's about damn time you got around to calling

me. Things can't be that exciting at the ranch that you don't have time to even say hello to me."

"Don't count on that."

"They're only cows, bro. Unless you did like Dylan and Sean and hooked up with women and trouble before you even climbed into a saddle."

"Well, there is this woman, Julie Gillespie, and she attracts danger like a field of wildflowers collects bees."

"And I'm guessing she's sexy, young, smart and sassy."

"All of the above."

"You guys are killing me. I am going to have to pay a visit to Mustang Run soon. For now, lay it out for me and don't leave out any of the pertinents."

Tyler explained the situation as succinctly as he could.

"Sheriff Grayson sounds like a player to me. Wouldn't trust him with a mangy hound dog, so take everything he says with a grain of margarita salt. Zeke Hartwell has never shown up on our radar, but dozens like him have. Doesn't fit the usual serial killer profile, though. I'd say he's more of a crime-of-opportunity type, especially against women or people weaker than himself."

"Which fits in the case of Muriel Frost," Tyler noted. "He'd been working on her house which was ten miles past nowhere."

"Exactly, and he sounds like the kind of cowardly rat who wouldn't hesitate to try to scare Julie off without showing his face."

"Makes sense," Tyler said.

"But that doesn't mean he's guilty. You need a lot more evidence than just opportunity."

"So what should be my next move, other than not leaving Julie unprotected?"

"Keep your eyes and ears open. Don't take chances. Carry a gun with enough power to get the job done."

"I have one in my car. How hard is it to get a permit to carry a concealed weapon in Texas?"

"For someone with your weapon experience? Call Glenn McGuire, explain it's an emergency. He'll issue it effective immediately."

"Did you forget that I'm the son of a convicted murderer?"

"You're a serviceman on leave, one who's been putting his life on the line daily in one of the most violent places on earth. McGuire will go with that if for no other reason than he won't like the idea of anyone in his county getting threatened like that, especially a woman.

"In the meantime, I'll shake a few trees and see what falls," Wyatt continued. "If I can get hold of Mom's and Muriel Frost's ME reports, I can see if the similarities in the attacks indicate a high probability of their being committed by the same perp. And you stick to Julie like she's cotton candy and you're the stick."

"Easy enough."

"Be careful, Tyler. I know you're used to danger, but be careful all the same. Sometimes the enemy can look like your best friend, and I don't want to lose a brother now that it looks like we might be on the path to being a family again."

"I have no intention of getting killed."

"Good. Keep me posted."

When the connection broke, Tyler finished his beer and went to search for Julie.

"Give me a minute," she called at his first tap on her bedroom door.

He wondered what she'd do if he pounced on her and kissed her senseless when she opened the door.

Instead, she knocked him senseless. He took a step backward and gulped for air.

"Wow! You look...different. Stunning, but different."

"Do you approve?"

"Oh, yeah, as long as it's not going to become the norm. I mean, you're a knockout. But I like the other you. The one with the shorts and ponytail and..." He touched the tip of her nose. "Less goop."

"It's just for tonight," she said. "But I do like to get dressed up on occasion."

"You clean up real well, but what's the occasion?"

"The festival dance. You did ask me to go with you, remember?"

"Oh, no. Is this the night?"

"It's Thursday."

"Give me twenty minutes. I'll be back." He reached up and twined a finger in one of the curly tendrils at her cheek. He hadn't planned it, but his mouth found hers and he went weak. If he didn't pull away quick, they'd never get to the dance.

"I'll be right back," he said. "And forget what I said about the goop. You look and taste divine."

JULIE TOUCHED HER FINGERTIPS to her lips and felt the heat from Tyler's kiss. In spite of the problems with the investigation, in spite of the threats, she had a feeling it would be a dynamite night.

ZEKE HARTWELL OPENED THE DOOR and slid into the front seat of his car. He'd found the perfect parking spot, only a block from the park where the festival was in full swing. He'd squeezed in between some paneled catering trucks where no one would see him come and go.

They were all busy selling their wares to the hicks who'd come out to celebrate a bunch of blue flowers that clogged every roadside and ditch between here and Dallas.

But he was in luck. He'd spotted his victim, hanging onto Tyler Ledger as if she was afraid he'd escape like one of those helium-filled balloons floating above them. She probably thought he could protect her. Imagine the shock when she found out he couldn't.

For eighteen years, he'd walked around a free man. Now she thought she'd just walk in and make a name for herself at his expense.

Julie Gillespie. A nobody who was too stupid to heed a direct threat when it came with photographic proof of what he was capable of.

He reached for the bottle of whiskey he'd stashed under his seat. He put it to his mouth and gulped, relishing the burn. But one good drink was all he could have tonight. He had to be thinking clearly when he made his move.

He didn't dread what he had to do. This wasn't the

way it had been with Muriel when the urge had come over him so suddenly he'd lost all control. And then when he could have taken her like a dog in heat, he'd become impotent. Attacked for nothing. Killed for frustration.

Tonight wasn't about lust.

It was about survival.

His.

Chapter Nine

Stars twinkled like diamonds above them as Julie and Tyler grazed their way past the rows of food booths sampling everything from deep fried meatballs in jalapeño butter to homemade tamales.

Tyler licked his fingers after finishing off a marinated steak shish kebab. "I will never be able to eat another army-issued MRE again without thinking of this food."

"One more hot pepper and my stomach may balk against ever eating again."

"You're in Texas now, baby. You have to learn to take the heat."

"Then I'll need lots of frozen margaritas to wash it down." She stirred the one she was holding and took another sip.

"I didn't expect so many people when Mustang Run is such a small town."

"It's probably not as small as you think. Residents are scattered on ranches and farms along every side road you pass coming in. And a lot of these people here tonight are from neighboring towns."

A strolling mariachi band walked by a few yards to their right, the music blending with laughter and talk and children's excited squeals as they rode one of the half-dozen carnival rides at the far end of the park.

"I'm glad I'm not the only one in a long Western skirt," Julie said.

"But you are the most ravishing"

"And like Collette said, I could have worn anything and still fit in."

There were sundresses with sandals, cocktail dresses with stiletto heels, and lots of jeans and skirts paired with fancy Western shirts atop the traditional cowboy boots.

Attire for the men was just as diverse, but Julie was certain no one looked as handsome as Tyler. She clearly wasn't the only one who thought that. She'd noticed more than one female festival goer cut her eyes and smile seductively when they passed.

"The only one getting more attention than you tonight might be me," Tyler said.

"I've noticed, but don't let it go to your head, cowboy."

"I'm talking about the glares followed by all the whispering. Like that couple in front of us in the beer line."

Julie turned to see who he was talking about. Just as Tyler said, the man was glaring at Tyler as if he'd just crashed a private party.

"It's only because they don't know you or Troy," Julie said.

"Don't worry. I can handle a few stares."

She slipped her arm around his waist, but jerked her hand away when her fingers touched cold metal beneath his light jacket.

"Can you legally carry that?"

"Yes. But I don't plan to need it. Relax. You need this night."

But not if it was going to put them both at undue risk.

"We don't have to stay."

"What? And have me miss my chance to dance with the prettiest woman in Mustang Run? We're staying, at least until the fireworks start."

But the anticipation she'd felt earlier began to wither. Everything she did put Tyler in danger. He could have had that in the war zone.

She couldn't back down now. It was her one chance to put the past behind her and go on with her life. But the costs should only extend to her.

"Uncle Tyler. Wait for us."

Julie turned to see Joey running across the grass in their direction. She wanted to shout at him to stay away, that being anywhere near her could be risky at best. But they were in the midst of hundreds of revelers. What could possibly go wrong?

"I rode the Tilt-A-Whirl and the Ferris wheel and I wasn't afraid at all. But I wasn't tall enough to ride the Inverter. And look what I won at the goldfish pond."

Julie bent down to examine this treasured prize, a plastic airplane that would probably not last the night. "Wow. Cool."

Eve stepped closer to Julie. "You look fantastic. The fabric in that skirt is exquisite. Where did you find it?"

"I don't remember," Julie lied. "It's not new. Are you staying for the dance?"

"Ugg. Dancing," Joey said. "What fun is that?"

"There's your answer," Sean said. "I think we're headed for the Moonwalk and then the funnel cake I've been waiting for all evening. But Dylan and Collette are in the dance tent somewhere. She'll be taking pictures all night."

Eve took Julie's hand and squeezed it as they started to walk away. "Take care, Julie. And thanks for that talk you had with Troy the other night. It meant a lot to him that you understood."

"And to me," she admitted.

"What kind of talk did you have with Troy?" Tyler asked.

"One about love and forgiveness."

"If we're going to dance, let's do it," he said, dropping the subject as if it were toxic.

He was back in Mustang Run, but he and his father were still miles and miles apart.

COMING TO THE DANCE HAD BEEN Tyler's idea, but with the band only halfway through its second set, he was starting to wish he'd never suggested it. Cradling Julie in his arms while they swayed to the Western band was tantalizing, but it only made him want more.

Besides, the crowds were too large and too fluid. He couldn't watch everyone at once. And even in a friendly crowd like this, he couldn't be sure the lunatic who had left the picture on Julie's car wouldn't strike.

"What do you say we get out of here and go back to the ranch?" he suggested.

"Fine by me. I'd like to dance with you without the gun," she whispered.

"How about without anything," he teased.

"Not even your boots."

"Well that might be overstepping things a bit."

A flash half blinded them just as they reached the edge of the portable dance floor.

"Best looking couple on the floor," Collette announced. "That skirt looks so elegant on you, Julie. Weren't you the one who said you had nothing to wear?"

Dylan stepped up behind Collette and circled her waist with his arms. "Haven't I heard *you* say that before, too, my gorgeous bride, who had to have an extra large closet of her own."

The conversation was interrupted by a shrill squeak from the stage mike. A plump woman in a red sequined vest cleared her throat and began to talk.

"I want to thank all of you who are here tonight for helping make this year's Bluebonnet Festival a huge success. And, remember, we still have three more days of fun. Every year gets bigger and better and we couldn't do it without you."

A light applause followed the announcement.

"Wait, there's more. I expect a really big round of applause for the board member who got the ball rolling by bidding the largest amount ever paid for a single item at the silent auction held last evening at Gilman's Steak House.

"Mr. Guy Cameron bid $22,000 for a handmade, one-of-a-kind, stained-glass window titled 'Bluebonnets in Bloom.' The window was donated by Steven Pate of Crowley's Fine Arts, right here in Mustang Run."

The crowd burst into applause.

"Guy, would you join me on the stage for a special presentation? And, Steven, if you're here, come on up, as well."

Tyler stayed glued to his spot not twenty feet from the stage. He wouldn't dare give up this chance to check out Guy Cameron, not after his wife had driven all the way to Willow Creek Ranch to share her thoughts on Muriel's murder with Julie.

Guy waved to the crowd like a politician as he made his way to the center of the stage. Tyler would guess him to be in his mid-fifties with salt-and-pepper hair and wearing jeans, a sport coat that had probably not come off the rack and a pair of what appeared to be hand-stitched alligator boots. The boots had no doubt come with a price tag to rival Guy's magnanimous bid.

The man reeked of charisma and the kind of confidence that comes from knowing he could buy and sell ninety-nine percent of his audience.

"I photographed his bird dogs for him once," Collette whispered. "Guy was super nice, but his wife was a real pain. She kept trying to tell me how to do my job, everything from the backdrop right down to the lighting. I would have walked off the job if the dogs hadn't been such delightful subjects."

Steven Pate never made it to the stage and Guy kept his thanks to under two minutes for the plaque he was presented.

"It's good to see you two," Tyler said to Dylan and Collette as Guy made his way off the stage. "But we're ready to call it a night."

"Lucky you," Dylan said. "I'm going to hang out here until Collette's through so I can drive her home. But I could use a break from the music. I'll walk to the car with you."

"Why don't you ride back to the ranch with them?" Collette suggested. "I may not be able to leave until midnight and I'm perfectly capable of driving myself home."

"But if I left you, who would keep the wolves in cowboy clothing at bay?"

"Okay. Stick around, lover boy. I'll save the last dance for you."

Julie turned to go and caught the heel of her dress boot in one of the electrical wires that snaked across the grass at the edge of the dance floor. Tyler tried to catch and steady her before she went tumbling to the ground. He missed and she fell smack into the arms of Guy Cameron.

"I'm sorry," she said, quickly righting herself.

Guy said nothing. He just stood there, staring down at Julie. His face turned a pasty white. His lips parted as if he were trying to speak and couldn't.

Tyler put a hand on Guy's arm. "Are you all right?"

Guy nodded, never taking his eyes off Julie.

"I hope I didn't puncture your foot with my heel," she said.

"No," he finally answered. "I'm glad I was there to break your fall. Have we met?"

"No. I'm Julie Gillespie."

"The reporter?" He sounded surprised, or maybe downright dumbfounded.

"Yes. Your wife came to the ranch where I'm staying to talk to me about the case. She must have told you."

"No. She didn't mention it."

Which was odd and this whole situation was starting to get a bit freaky. Tyler put a possessive arm around Julie's waist and extended his free hand to Guy. "I'm Tyler Ledger. Sorry for the way we met, but nice to meet you."

"One of the Ledgers of Willow Creek Ranch?" Guy asked.

"I'm Troy's son." So make something of it, if you think you're tough enough, he added silently.

Guy took Tyler's hand. "Why don't the two of you join Candice and me for a drink?"

"Another time," Tyler said. "We were leaving when Julie stumbled."

Guy only nodded, his former charisma as dull as yesterday's email.

"What was that about?" Dylan asked as he and Tyler followed Collette and Julie to the edge of the crowd.

"Hell if I know, but I intend to find out."

"When you do, I'd like to hear about it."

Dylan walked on the opposite side of Julie as they headed to the car. Tyler realized his brother was intentionally helping him form a protective circle around her though his car was parked in the nearest lot and there were sizeable crowds still perusing the area.

The evening's fireworks display got underway just as they reached the lot. A cacophony of explosions echoed around them. All eyes went heavenward as the brilliant starbursts filled the skies and a chorus of oohs and aahs replaced the talk and laughter.

They stopped near the car to enjoy the visual extravaganza. The popping sounds made Tyler even more nervous. Who'd know if a gun was fired?

"Get in the car, Julie."

"Then I couldn't see the show."

Something whizzed by Tyler's head and ricocheted of the door of his rented car.

"Gunfire. Get down," he yelled, shoving Julie to the ground and falling on top of her.

Julie yelped in pain. And then Tyler saw the streak of blood stretching across the front window of the car.

Chapter Ten

Julie stared at Tyler, his frame backlit by vibrant sprays of red, green and blue. He was helping her up with one hand. His other held a gun.

Dylan was leaning against the car and blood was running down his arm.

Julie's heart slammed against the walls of her chest as she finally grasped what had happened.

"Oh, my god, Dylan. You've been shot."

The few strangers who realized what had happened began to crowd around them, all talking at once.

"It's nothing, just a flesh wound," Dylan said to no one in particular. He lifted his bleeding arm to prove his point.

"We need an ambulance," someone called.

"I'm calling 9-1-1," a man holding a cell phone to his ear assured them.

"I saw a guy running off between those flagpoles on the other side of the parking lot," a woman said, her voice edging on hysterics. "I think he was the sniper."

Tyler opened the car door and started pushing Julie

inside. Stabs of pain radiated from her left ankle all the way up her leg. But there was no blood on her.

Tyler took a closer look at Dylan's arm. "Are you sure you're okay?"

"I'm good."

"Then stick with Julie. And call Sheriff McGuire. He already knows about the threats."

Tyler disappeared into the crowd. Julie jumped from the car to go after him. Dylan grabbed her and pushed her between him and the car.

"Then you go after him, Dylan! Stop Tyler before he gets shot!"

"You heard what he said. He wants me here with you."

"I don't need you. Tyler does. Please go with him."

"Take it easy. You're drawing a crowd."

As if she cared. She tried to break from Dylan's hold, but even hurt, he was too strong for her.

This was all her fault. This was her fight. But it was Dylan who'd been shot and Tyler was chasing a sniper.

Her hardheadedness might get them all killed.

TYLER CUT ACROSS THE PARKING lot and raced past the flagpoles, constantly scanning for any sign of the shooter. Some kids on bikes were riding in the middle of the road. A man walking a poodle crossed the street. He yelled at them all to clear the area.

Tyler jumped to the top of a panel bakery truck for a better look at the surroundings. The crunch of tires and the squeal of brakes grabbed his attention. He turned, just as a car backed from between two trucks, turned and took the corner on two wheels before speeding out of sight.

The disappointment of defeat crashed down on him like a wall of rocks. So much for his ability as a protector. The guy had missed Julie by inches.

Two deputies ran toward him as he jumped down from the roof of the vehicle."

"He's heading west in a black car," Tyler yelled.

"I'll call for a patrol search," one of the deputies yelled. "We'll take it from here."

But they were too late to do anything about the sniper. He was long gone.

Dylan was sitting on the front fender of Tyler's rental car talking to Sheriff McGuire when Tyler made it back to them. Collette was standing next to Dylan, leaning on his good arm and holding tight.

Julie was still sitting in the car. She made no move to get out.

"I take it you didn't find the sniper," McGuire said.

"I saw him drive off, but I was too late to stop him."

The two deputies who'd chased after Tyler joined them. "I called in the location to headquarters," one of them said.

"Good work. From here on out, this is our responsibility, Tyler. We're dealing with a man who's armed and dangerous."

"I second that," Collette said. "I'm taking Dylan to the emergency room."

Dylan shrugged. "I told her it's nothing. She won't listen."

"*Nothing* would be if we didn't have reporters stirring up trouble and getting you shot at," Collette protested.

"This isn't Julie's fault," Tyler said. "If you have to blame anyone, Collette, then blame me."

"I do," Collette said furiously. "In the future, just leave my husband out of your stunts."

Dylan put his good arm around his wife's shoulder. "I think I'd best get Collette out of here."

"Go ahead," McGuire said. "I know where to find you if I have more questions. I need you to stick around for a few more minutes, Tyler."

The sheriff asked several questions, most of which Tyler had answered when they'd talked by phone earlier that night.

"I'm having second thoughts about issuing you that concealed weapons permit, Tyler."

"I've probably had more experience with firearms than all your deputies combined."

"Which is why I agreed to your request. But I don't like the idea of private citizens taking over the jobs my department should be able to handle. How much longer are you planning to be in Mustang Run?"

"Six more days."

"Then stop by my office tomorrow. I'll deputize you. But don't expect any pay. This is just to make you legal."

"You may get some static for deputizing one of Troy Ledger's sons."

"I get static if a cow finds a broken fence and wanders onto the road. Besides I'm not deputizing Troy. I'm deputizing you, a loyal member of the U.S. Army."

McGuire started to walk away but stopped and shook a short, pudgy finger at Tyler. "But don't take any foolish risks. I don't want any private citizen caught in a cross fire."

"Neither would I."

When McGuire left, Tyler slid beneath the car's steering wheel. Julie didn't say a word.

He leaned toward her and let his head rest against hers. "Guess I'm a lousy bodyguard."

"You're not a bodyguard, Tyler. You're just a super nice guy who got caught up in my problems. If I hadn't insisted on defying the threats, none of this would have happened."

"Does that mean you're giving up the case?"

"No. It means that I have to leave Willow Creek Ranch before I tear all of your lives apart and mine, as well."

"Do we have to start this again tonight? We're both too tired and frustrated for this kind of discussion."

"Fine. We won't discuss it."

She closed her eyes tight and a lone tear escaped to trail down her cheek. Tyler kissed it away, and then kissed her hard on the mouth, not coming up for air until he could feel her frustration melting away.

Tonight had taken a toll on her, but she wasn't even close to giving up her search for the truth in the Frost murder case. That's why he had to work fast. He had six days left to find and stop the man who'd fired that bullet tonight.

He wouldn't leave Julie unprotected, not even if it meant...

AWOL.

The possibility of that was as impossible as leaving her to face a killer on her own.

The clock was ticking. He had to work fast.

JULIE WINCED IN PAIN AS SHE stepped out of the car.

Tyler jumped from the vehicle. "What's wrong?"

"I must have sprained my left ankle when you were trying to shield me from sniper fire."

She took a step. "I can walk. It just smarts."

Tyler rushed around the hood, crouched and lifted the red skirt. "It's swollen. We better get some ice on it."

"It's not crip…" Her words were swallowed by a moan as she tried to take another step only to have to lean on him for support.

Tyler scooped her up and kicked the car door closed behind them. The skirt billowed over his arms and caught the evening breeze as he carried her up the steps and to the door.

The door was unlocked. He'd rectify that tonight. Even the ranch couldn't serve as a haven now.

The light in the family room was on, but the house was desolately quiet.

He suspected Dylan had not called Troy to fill him in on the night's close call. If he had, Troy would be up waiting for news.

Tyler carried Julie to her bedroom door. She turned the knob and pushed it open.

The curtains at the sliding glass door had been left open. Filtered moonlight painted silver streaks across the antique dresser and added an eerie glow to the bed's reflection in the mirror.

Tyler crossed the worn hooked rug and threw back the blue and white quilt, settling Julie atop the crisp white sheets. He bent and kissed her. One salty sweet taste of her and the defeating fatigue he'd dealt with on the drive back to the ranch evaporated.

He only hoped the kiss did as much for her and that she didn't start in again about leaving the ranch.

"Don't move," he said. "I'll be right back with an ice pack." He picked up a pillow, fluffed it and placed it under her swollen and bruising ankle. "What else can I get you?"

"A glass of cold water."

"How about a chaser of peppermint schnapps?"

"That might help," she admitted.

"I'll be right back."

He didn't locate a legitimate ice pack, so he filled a plastic zip bag with ice and wrapped it in a clean terry kitchen towel. He took down glasses for the water and liqueur and even found a tray to carry it all.

By the time he'd returned to the bedroom, Julie had wiggled out from the skirt and blouse and was working on unclasping her lacy white bra.

His need for her hit so fast and hard that the tray shook in his hands, rattling the glasses. "You started without me. No fair."

The clasp released and she yanked off the bra and tossed it to the floor. In the next move she covered herself with the sheet. "I think we should talk, Tyler."

"Talk. With you naked?"

"I'm serious."

"So am I. Don't you know that *We should talk* are the three scariest words in the English language. Ask any man."

"Our making love tonight won't change anything. It won't change the situation. It won't change us."

He fit the towel-covered ice around her ankle. "Neither will my sleeping alone while I ache to hold you in my arms."

"You make this so difficult, Tyler."

"It doesn't have to be." He kicked off his boots and lay down beside her. "I don't take making love to you lightly, Julie. I've never met anyone like you, never met a woman who I trusted the way I do you."

"Then let me be part of you. Talk to me about the real you. What you think. What you believe. Why you keep so much bottled inside you."

"I'm not sure I can."

"At least try."

Tyler sat down on the edge of the mattress. This time when the memories slipped from their carefully guarded mental lockboxes, he let them. "I don't know who I am, Julie. I spent my life being manipulated by other people's needs and fears. 'Hate your father. Love your mother. Pretend to like living with Aunt Sibley. Pretend you hated your life on the ranch. Forget you had brothers, unless we tell you it's time to see them.' There was no end to the pretense."

"Then it's time you start finding out what you feel and what you need."

"Right now, I need you." He lay down beside her and

kissed her again. This time the tremors of anticipation were shared and she lifted the sheets and invited him closer.

He kissed her forehead, her eyes, her nose and mouth and kept going. When he reached her breasts, he cuddled, licked, nibbled and sucked.

Finally he slipped his hand inside her panties and explored until he found the spot that made her tremble and moan in pleasure.

"These have to go," he said. He removed the scrap of white lace panties and then crawled out of the bed to undress himself.

Julie threw her good leg over the edge of the bed and dragged the other one behind it.

"What do you think you're doing?"

She pressed her good foot to the floor. "Hobbling to the bathroom."

"I'll carry you."

"That's going a bit above and beyond."

"I don't know why. It's not like I thought you were exempt from bodily functions," he teased.

"Okay, help me in there," she agreed.

He did and while she took care of business he shed his clothes. He opened the small drawer in the bedside table so that he could put the gun in it. That would keep it out of sight, but near at hand.

A snapshot of Julie in her red skirt and white blouse caught his eye. He pulled it out for a closer look. It was the same skirt, the same—or almost the same—blouse. It was even the same hairdo.

It was not Julie.

"You can help me back to bed," Julie said.

He looked from the picture to her.

"Who is this?"

She stared at him, staying silent until he asked again.

"Who's the woman in this photograph?"

"That's Muriel."

"Muriel Frost?"

"Yes. I found it in the attic at the old farmhouse."

"She's wearing the same outfit you wore tonight, and you look so much like her, I thought it was you."

"I know."

Julie hobbled toward the bed and took a deep breath. "And Muriel looks exactly like my mother did at that age." Her voice grew weedy thin. "They were twins."

Tyler struggled to make sense of what she was saying. "Are you telling me that you're Muriel Frost's niece?"

She nodded. "I'm the little girl who was afraid to talk."

Tyler reached for his jeans. "So you've been lying to me all along."

ONCE BACK TO THE BED, JULIE hugged the sheet around her naked body while Tyler wiggled back into his jeans. He reached to the floor and picked up the ice pack that had somehow been knocked to the floor. And in a room consumed by tension and angst, Tyler carefully wrapped the ice pack back around her ankle.

His thoughtfulness multiplied the guilt she felt for keeping so much from him.

Tyler stood at the foot of the bed, clutching the ornate post. "Did you see your aunt beaten and murdered?"

"Not beaten," Julie said. "Or if I did see that I blocked it completely from my mind. I remember slinking out of my bedroom and crouching behind the upstairs banister. And I remember the shots." She put her hands over her ears. "I can still hear them when I think about that day."

"Do you remember anything about the man?"

"I remember that he was big and that he had greasy hair that hung down in his face."

"That's all."

"I was seven years old and scared. My mother had just been murdered at work. And now a guy with a gun had just shot and killed my aunt. I doubt I was searching for identifying marks."

Just stay calm, though he certainly wasn't, at least not on the inside. "So you never were able to give any kind of description to the police?"

"That's what it says in the police report and what was printed in newspaper accounts at the time. Supposedly I was traumatized into an almost comalike state. All I remember are the shots and being inside that house with my dead aunt for what seemed like days, hiding under my bed in case the man came back."

"The police file said it was only a matter of hours until the body was found," Tyler said.

"It seemed days to me."

"What happened after that?"

"I was placed in a series of foster homes. Each worse than the one before. Miraculously, a single woman, a retired teacher, adopted me when I was twelve. That's when I became Julie Gillespie instead of Lenora Frost. She died instantly of a brain aneurysm when I was sixteen. Under no circumstances was I going back into foster care, so I stole some money she kept at the house, moved from Beaumont, Texas, to New Orleans and set out on my own."

"How did you support yourself?"

"Working for anyone who would hire me. I washed dishes, waitressed, worked the night shift in twenty-four-hour liquor stores. I did everything but prostitute myself and I considered that a time or two. In the meantime, I managed to earn my GED and pick up a few journalism credits at UNO. That gave me the nerve and the know-how to start my column. You know the rest."

"So everything you told me about being a spoiled rotten only child was lies?" Accusation smoked his eyes and made his voice edgy.

"I liked to think of it as erecting a protective shell."

"That you kept up, even after we kissed. And made love. And you would have kept on with the lies if I hadn't found that picture tonight."

His disappointment in her cut deep. "I did what I had to do, Tyler. Surely you can understand that. If I'd come here as the niece of Muriel Frost, I'd have had zero clout. Sheriff Grayson definitely wouldn't have turned over the police records to me. I seriously doubt Candice Cameron would have come to me with her story.

"Even Muriel's friend, Kara Saunders, would have blown me off. In fact she did, when I was only sixteen and sought her out. I was desperate for answers about the nightmares that haunt me to this day. She said I should forget the past and move on with my life, that asking too many questions could be dangerous. That's when I first began to think that there was some kind of cover-up involved in the case."

"So you kept your fake identity and moved into the Ledger home. My brothers and Collette warned me then that I shouldn't trust you. I ignored them."

Tyler let go of the bedpost and started to pace. "You were hoping Troy would be involved, weren't you? You probably still are. It would make your story that much more intriguing."

"I never hoped that, and it was never about the story."

"Bullshit!"

Julie fought the tears, but the fight that had kept her going all her life surfaced, too. "You think you have the corner on trust issues, Tyler Ledger? Well, you don't. All my life, I've been kicked in the teeth every time I tried to get up. But I still put myself out there. If I had a father who was reaching out to me, I'd at least go halfway to meet him."

"I don't see you forgiving the man who killed your aunt."

"Troy didn't kill your mother."

"You can't possibly know that."

"I can and you'd know it, too, if you talked to him and really let yourself listen to what he says. He loved your mother with the kind of love you may never even be able to understand. He loves her still. No matter what happens to him for the rest of his life, that will never change."

Tyler quit pacing. "I didn't come in here to talk about Troy." He walked back to the bed and sat on the edge of the mattress, the weight of his body tilting her toward him.

"I don't want to talk about this anymore tonight. And I want no more talk about your leaving the ranch. You could have been killed tonight. I can't let that happen."

She swallowed hard, fighting the tears. "If protection is all you have to give, I don't want it."

"Don't, Julie. I need time. I…"

"Get out, Tyler. Please. Just go."

She turned over and buried her face in the pillow to muffle the sobs she could no longer hold.

Her emotions were too raw even for her to fully understand, but she knew that it was over for her and Tyler. Even if she'd been honest from the very beginning, there would have been never a happy ending.

She'd always known that. So why did hearing it in his voice and seeing it in his eyes hurt so much?

JULIE JERKED AWAKE, SHIVERING and freezing cold. She sat up quickly, rubbing her tear-swollen eyes and checking to see if the door to the garden had been left open.

The curtain was closed and unmoving, yet an icy draft swept over her body and lifted the hairs on the back of her neck. Her teeth chattered as she pulled the quilt to her neck. Nothing helped. The frost was bone deep.

An eerie shadow moved across the bed accompanied

by a whispery sound like the rustle of silk. Fingers locked with hers. A ghostly figure coalesced over her bed.

She tried to scream. There was only silence.

She was lost in a nightmare and couldn't wake up.

Chapter Eleven

"Don't be afraid, Julie. I'm not here to hurt you."

The voice was ethereal, like music coming from her soul. "Who are you?" Julie whispered. "What do you want?"

"To warn you."

"Warn me of what?"

"The evil that is searching for you. It is coming for you just as it came for Muriel."

This wasn't real. It wasn't happening. Julie would wake up and the presence would vaporize and disappear.

Instead gossamer tatters of white swirled about the room.

"What evil?" Julie begged. "I must know what to watch for."

"You will know. Don't let it destroy you. My son needs you."

Julie lay perfectly still, rapt by the ghostly essence that darted about the room, disappearing only to change shape and then recreate itself again. "Are you talking about Tyler?"

"Yes. My son needs you. He needs his father. You must stay alive."

"Make me know you're real, Helene. Give me a sign."

"The sign is love."

"Your son doesn't love me."

"You must help him learn how."

Ribbons of color danced across the ceiling. "Take care, Julie. Don't let evil win. Muriel will help you find the answers you need. So will Guy."

"Help me how?"

"Trust your instincts and you'll know."

The image disappeared and the room became so hot Julie thought it must be on fire. She kicked off the covers, then moaned as pain burned red hot in her ankle.

But just as suddenly the room cooled back to normal. The draft died. The frigid cold had burned off.

Helene's ghost was gone.

But humans only talked to ghosts in fiction and fantasy. If the paranormal world existed at all, it never intermingled with reality. It had only been a nightmare brought on by the sniper attack and the emotional meltdown with Tyler.

Or maybe, it was just Julie's subconscious reminding her that she hadn't finished what she'd come here to do.

There was evil in the form of the sniper who'd fired on her tonight. Evil had come looking for her.

But how could Muriel help her? And Guy?

Julie's mind drifted back to Guy Cameron and the way he'd looked at her tonight.

Could he have been more than Muriel's boss?

Had he and Muriel been having an affair?

What help could he possibly offer?

She had to talk to him, face-to-face, demand answers. But she wouldn't ask Tyler to drive her there. She'd just have to suck up the pain and drive herself. Luckily, it was the left foot that she'd strained.

Beware of the evil. But how dangerous could it be to visit Guy Cameron in his office? He was a successful businessman. It wasn't as if he could just kill her and wrap her up in a rug.

First thing in the morning, she'd make that call.

JULIE WOKE AS EXHAUSTED AS if she'd been jogging Hill Country hiking paths all night. She'd lain awake for two hours after the ghostly nightmare, straining to hear any strange sound and watching for any unexplained movement.

When she'd finally fallen asleep, her dreams had been haunted by memories of the scene with Tyler. They'd both been overwrought from the sniper incident and she'd thrown him some pretty serious curves when she'd explained her true identity.

Perhaps getting it all out in the open had been for the best, but she still didn't like the thought of leaving things that way. She slid out of bed and gingerly tried a bit of weight on the ankle. The pain was not nearly as severe as it had been last night and some of the swelling had gone down.

Hobbling was doable as long as she took it slow. She made it from the bed to the dresser and then to the closet for her luggage.

She'd brought little with her. It wouldn't take long to pack. But before she got started, she'd make that call to Guy Cameron.

It took five minutes of hold time before his secretary finally put her though to him.

"Mr. Cameron, this is Julie Gillespie. We met last night at the Bluebonnet Festival."

"Yes, I remember. What can I do for you?"

"I'd really like to talk to you."

"I'm listening."

"What I want to talk about could be better done in person, today if possible."

"I'll have to put you on hold while I check my schedule for the day."

"I'll hold. I won't take much of your time, but it's important that we talk as soon as possible."

His checking took only a matter of seconds.

"How about two o'clock this afternoon in my Austin office?"

"Perfect."

"I'll put my secretary on again and she can give you directions."

"I'd appreciate that."

"But I should warn you, Miss Gillespie, that everything I know about Muriel Frost's murder, I told to Sheriff Grayson years ago. So if you're hoping for deep, dark secrets, you'll be disappointed."

That was exactly what she was hoping for. And she

had leverage to secure them. She had a feeling Guy Cameron would be shocked once again.

"Come alone," he said. "I never deal with reporters who travel in packs. And no photographers, not even Collette."

"You got it."

That done, only the packing remained. When she finished what she had to do today, and when she drove away from Willow Creek Ranch for the last time, she'd put the past completely behind her.

WHY WAS FIGHTING A WAR SO much easier than maintaining a relationship with a woman?

The mental question was rhetorical. Tyler knew he couldn't answer it.

And yet, when Julie had suggested he go with her to the horse barn to see Guinevere, he'd jumped at the chance. He needed to apologize for the things he'd said in anger last night. He might even have to beg her forgiveness. He would, if it came to that.

There was no way he could let her go through with her threat to leave the ranch today, not with a killer on the loose.

He'd been in many a battle over the last four years. Some scary as hell. All with the potential for fatalities. But he'd never known the kind of panic he'd felt last night when he'd seen the blood on the car and thought she'd been hit.

Julie limped to the back steps from the table where they'd just finished a plate of Troy's famous hotcakes.

"The ankle doesn't hurt the way it did last night, but I'll still have to move slow," Julie reminded him.

She hobbled down the one step. There were two more to go.

"Wait," he teased, though his heart wasn't in it. "I better go back and pack a lunch. This could take all day."

"Okay, I'll do it on my own."

"I have a better idea." He bent over. "If you won't ride a real horse, try this one out for size, but no spurs allowed."

"You can't ride me piggyback all the way to the barn."

"Sure I can," he said. "I tote backpacks that weigh more than you over rocky mountain trails. The army doesn't tolerate wimps. Climb aboard."

"Are you sure?"

"I never offer what I'm not sure I want to give. Come on. Wrap your legs around my waist and let's go."

She finally gave in. Crazy but he liked the feel of her bouncing along on his back with those great legs of hers wrapped around his waist. And she was lighter than some of the packs he had to carry on mountainous missions.

The barn door was open. A wasp buzzed around the entrance. Tyler swatted it away and carried Julie inside, setting her down next to Guinevere's stall.

"You two are up early," Collette called from the back of the barn. She flicked her sleeve across her forehead to bat away a fly.

"So are you," Tyler said. "I thought you might sleep in today and let one of the wranglers take care of your chores."

"I missed Guinevere. So what's with the piggy-backing?"

"I sprained an ankle," Julie said. "Tyler was playing knight in shining armor."

"Actually I sprained it for her," Tyler said, "so I owed her the ride."

"How did you sprain her ankle?"

"I was a bit overzealous in my body shielding technique," Tyler explained.

"Better sprained than shot," Julie said. "How's Dylan?"

"Fine. I tried to get him to sleep in this morning, but he was up with the sun, as usual."

"Can't keep a good man down," Tyler said. "Do you need some help with the horses?"

"Sure. How about taking over for me with getting their fresh water? I'll switch to the feeding routine."

"I can handle that."

"And I'm sorry for getting bent out of shape last night. I think the sniper incident was too close to my own brushes with danger. Anyway, I didn't mean the harsh accusations, Julie."

"I wouldn't blame you if you had," Julie said. "I have caused trouble for the Ledgers. I'm just glad Dylan was not seriously hurt last night."

"Me, too."

Tyler walked to the back and started filling pails

with water from the hose. Best to let the women talk. Collette's change in attitude might make persuading Julie to stay a dab easier.

JULIE HUNG ON GUINEVERE'S stall. "She's so adorable. I can see why you've grown so attached to her, Collette."

"I'm attached to all of my horses, but I'm pretty sure Guinevere will stay a favorite. Do you ride?"

"No," Julie answered quickly. "The adult horses are much too big for me. I'd never feel secure in the saddle."

"You'd learn. You just have to let your horse know who's boss. And you have to respect them. Remember those two things and you'll be fine."

"I may give it a try one day. But not yet."

"How are things going in the Ledger household? Are you sleeping okay?"

Julie wondered if she should be reading something into the question. "Shouldn't I be?"

"It's rumored to be haunted, you know."

"Yes, we talked about that the first night I was here. I don't believe in ghosts."

"Neither do I, but…"

Julie knew exactly what Collette was thinking. "I must confess that I woke up last night and the room was frigid." She'd lowered her voice so Tyler wouldn't hear her confession.

"The very same thing happened to me when I was sleeping there. And then it's like there's a presence in the room, a presence that is very protective of the Ledger sons."

Julie backed away, suddenly uncomfortable with the conversation. "You do know that it's probably just our overactive imaginations?"

"Absolutely," Collette agreed.

They were both lying.

"Troy said I'd probably find you here."

They all turned at the brusque male voice.

"Hope I'm not interrupting anything."

"Dad, what are you doing here?" Collette asked.

"I'm making a call in my official capacity as sheriff. A right pleasant call, I might add."

"In that case, it's a real pleasure to see you." Tyler turned off the hose and walked to where Sheriff McGuire was leaning against a roughhewn support post. "What's the news?"

"We now know the exact location of Zeke Hartwell."

Julie hobbled closer. "Where?"

"In my jail. We got a tip from a man out walking his dog last night. He gave us the license plate number of a guy he saw driving like a maniac away from the park. Said he thought the man might have stolen something from the catering trucks parked out back."

"What time was that?" Julie asked.

"Minutes after that bullet barely missed you. Deputies arrested him at a truck stop just this side of Austin. Guess he planned to lay low for a couple of days."

"What about the weapon?"

"He had several on him, none licensed to him. One stolen recently. We'll have to wait on a ballistics match from the FBI to see if one of the weapons fired the bullet that I recovered next to your car. But there's no doubt in my mind that Zeke's the man who left the threats and then tried to kill you."

"Which means he must be Muriel's killer," Julie said as the truth slowly sank in.

"I s'pect you're right, Julie. You're a hell of an investigative reporter. You'll go far."

She swallowed hard at the compliment. "Actually, I'm not sure that's the career for me, but right now I'm so happy I could cry."

Tears started rolling down her cheek to prove her point. "I just can't believe that Muriel's killer will finally face trial."

"Neither can I." Collette did a quick two-step with a pitchfork. "Celebration at my house. Everyone invited."

"You really don't need to do that," Julie protested.

"Of course, I do. Dad, you're expected. Oh, and we'll invite Bob Adkins and his wife. And naturally Sean and Eve, and Troy and Tyler. And Joey and Sparky. Who am I leaving out? I know," she answered herself. "I'll invite Abby."

"Does seven o'clock work for you, Julie?"

How could she say no, even though it would mean one more night sleeping in the same house as Tyler without touching him. And one more night with the ghost of Helene Ledger.

"Seven works," she agreed.

Collette left with her father, leaving Julie and Tyler alone with the horses.

He snaked an arm around her shoulders.

"You did it," he said. "And you were right. You didn't need me."

Nothing had ever been less true.

He kissed her, slow and sweet and frighteningly final. If there had been time, she might have taught Tyler to love just as Helene's ghost had said she should. But time had run out.

She'd go on with her life, whatever that turned out to be. Tyler would go back to active duty on the other side of the world.

A breaking heart left success painfully bittersweet.

GUY CAMERON STOOD AT THE plate glass window of his twenty-third-floor office and looked out at the city of Austin. For a kid who'd grown up stealing other kids' lunch money so he could buy milk for his baby brother, he'd come a long way.

He had all the trappings of luxury that money could buy. A house on Lake LBJ with a yacht docked at the marina. A condo in Cabo San Lucas. A six-bedroom cabin in Vail. And a mansion in the most exclusive section inside Austin city limits.

And he had a wife who lived on prescription drugs to keep her mental condition halfway stable. She had no idea of the sacrifices he'd made for her. He'd given Candice everything she wanted except love. He didn't have any love to give.

He hadn't really felt much of anything for eighteen years.

And then it had been for Muriel.

But it was the all grown-up version of Lenora Frost he

had to deal with now. He'd practically grown comatose when he'd seen her last night. It was as if Muriel had come back from the dead.

Only a close blood relative could look that much like Muriel. Only a niece with a mother who'd been Muriel's twin.

He wondered if given the same choices he'd had then, he'd make the same decisions. He'd never know. Candice's family inheritance had been a major temptation. He'd have never had the capital to wind up where he was now without it.

The phone on his desk buzzed.

He punched the speaker button.

"Miss Gillespie is here to see you."

"Good. Show her in. And why don't you take the rest of the afternoon off, Jerri? Start your weekend early. It's a gorgeous spring day, and I won't need you again before Monday."

"Why, thank you, Mr. Cameron. Enjoy your weekend."

Chapter Twelve

Julie limped to the proffered seat on an oversize leather sofa. Guy didn't sit, but rather walked over to stand near the window and divide his attention between her and the magnificent view.

"What is it you think I can help you with, Miss Gillespie?"

"I'd like to ask you a few questions about a former employee."

"I know who you are, Julie, so we can skip the part where you pretend to be an investigative reporter with no personal ties to Muriel Frost."

"I don't know what you're talking about."

"Sure you do. You're Muriel's niece, her only niece, the one who witnessed the murder. And you're here on some kind of quest for revenge and justice."

No use to fake it. It would be better this way. "How long have you known?"

"Since I saw you at the dance last night. So let's start over. Why did you insist on seeing me today?"

"I'm looking for closure."

Julie pulled the half photo from the side pocket of

her purse and handed it to him. "Do you remember the night this photo was taken?"

His hands shook. "Where did you get this?"

"Does it matter? All you need to know is that I have the other half in a safe place. I don't think you'd like for it to fall into the sheriff's hands."

He walked back to the window. "If it's money you want, Julie, we can work something out."

"I don't want your money, Guy. I just want the truth. If you give me that, I won't use the information to incriminate you, nor will I use it in an article. I give you my word on that."

"What is it you want to know?"

"Were you in love with Aunt Muriel?"

He dropped to his chair, put down the snapshot and buried his head in his hands for almost a minute before he looked her in the eye. "I was. We didn't mean for it to happen. It just did. There was no way not to love Muriel. She was fun to be with, made me feel like a king in the days when I had nothing. But she was also sweet and warm and giving."

"Did Candice know about your affair with Muriel?"

"No, but it was more than an affair. I was going to ask for a divorce. Muriel died before I could."

"And you never told the police about the affair?"

"If I had, they would have tried to pin the murder on Candice and I knew she didn't kill Muriel—I was sure she didn't kill her."

Only he couldn't have been sure. Julie would still think she might be guilty if she didn't know that Zeke had committed the horrid crime.

"I think you believe that Candice did kill her and you kept quiet so that you didn't lose her inheritance. I don't know how you've lived with yourself all these years, Guy. But you only fooled yourself. You were never really in love with Muriel or Candice. You were in love with you. I feel sorry for Candice for having wasted her life on a man who thinks she's capable of murder."

Guy opened his desk drawer. "I knew this was about money. Name your price, Julie. One hundred thousand? Two? I'll write you the check just to get rid of you."

"Go to hell, Guy Cameron."

Julie left the office, then took the elevator to the first floor, limping across the street to the coffee shop. Her insides were shaking. She had her closure, but it wasn't nearly as satisfying as she'd hoped.

The only good thing that would come of any of this was that Muriel's killer would finally stand trial.

CANDICE CAMERON HAD JUST PAID for her caramel latte when she spotted Julie Gillespie through the swinging door of the coffee shop. Irritation swept through her like a tidal wave. There was only one reason for her to be in this neighborhood.

She was here to see Guy.

She'd known the woman was trouble from the second Sheriff Grayson had told her that she'd been in his office asking all those questions.

Caleb Grayson had told her to make friends with Julie and frighten her into backing out of her investigation.

Well, she'd tried. It obviously hadn't worked.

Now it was time to get serious. There was far too much at stake to take chances now.

She stirred her coffee and plastered a smile on her face.

"Julie. What in the world are you doing in my part of town?"

Julie turned toward her and smiled. "I had some appointments nearby, so I decided to grab a coffee before driving home."

"It's such a coincidence to run into you," Candice crooned. "I was just about to call you."

"Really?"

Julie put in the order for her coffee and then limped her way over to Candice. "What did you want to talk to me about?"

"I was going through some things in one of the storage buildings we've had for years. Anyway, you'll never guess what I found."

"I'm sure I can't."

"Some scrapbooks and pictures that belonged to Muriel Frost. I must have rescued them from the vandals and then forgot I had them. Some are of her and her twin sister when they were still in high school. Did you know she had a twin?"

"I did."

"Right. I guess that would have shown up when you were doing all that research. Anyway I took the pictures to the old farmhouse where Muriel was living when she was killed."

"Why take them there?"

"To make it more convenient for you to pick them up.

I stuck them inside the drawer of the old rolltop desk. It's on the second floor. You can't miss it."

"Why would you think I'd go there?"

"To see the house, of course. I told Sheriff Grayson you could have anything you found there that might help you with your investigation. I figured you needed some human interest items to include in your article. He did give you the message, didn't he?"

"No, but I would love to have the pictures."

"Feel free to stop by there on your way home."

"I may do that."

"I notice you're limping. Are you okay?"

"It's just a sprain. I'll be fine."

"Good. But be careful in that old house. I've been saying for years that with the rotting walls and decaying floors, it's just a matter of time until someone gets killed in there."

TYLER HOPPED BACK INTO HIS truck to head back to Willow Creek Ranch after closing Sean's gate behind him. He'd spent the last few hours touring by pickup truck Sean's new horse farm and listening to some of the fascinating horse whisperer tales. He hadn't realized until today what an interesting life Sean had led.

There was a lot about all his brothers he didn't know.

That fact was the perfect example of what Julie had been trying to tell him. He had to give family life a chance if he expected to get anything from it.

He had five days left before his leave ended. It wasn't much time, but it was a place to start.

Julie was a very smart woman.

He'd goofed things up with her and now all she wanted to do was get away from the ranch and from him. He didn't really blame her. Trust was hard to come by when you had the kind of pasts they'd had.

She hadn't trusted him enough to tell him the truth. He hadn't trusted their feelings for each other to get them past the lies.

But when they'd made love, it had been paradise.

His cell phone rang. He grabbed it, hoping it was Julie though he wasn't really expecting her to call.

"Hello."

"Is this Tyler?"

"Yes, it is. And this sounds like big brother Wyatt."

"In the flesh. I know you said the murder mystery is solved, but I just got a copy of that ME report on Muriel Frost and I think you'll find it interesting."

"How's that?"

"She was four months' pregnant."

"I don't remember any reference to that in the police file."

"I knew you didn't say anything about it. Any idea who the father was?"

"Now that you mention it, I'd say it was Guy Cameron." The guy had been in love with Muriel Frost. What else could explain that reaction he had to Julie last night?

"I gotta run," Wyatt said. "I'm in the middle of a big case, but I thought I'd pass that on for what it's worth."

"I appreciate it."

"Any time. And next time you're going to be in the States, how about giving me a little advance warning? I'd like to make one of those family cookouts with the rest of you."

"I will definitely let you know."

Tyler tried to call Julie and tell her what about the pregnancy. There was no answer. He checked his messages just in case he'd missed one.

No voice messages but someone had sent a text. He pulled it up.

On my way to farmhouse crime scene. Be home after. Julie.

Anxiety started rolling in his gut. Why would she be going there?

There was one sure way to find out. He made a U-turn. If nothing else, someone should be there to stamp the roaches for her.

COMING TO THE FARMHOUSE ALONE no longer seemed a good idea. With Tyler, the house had seemed run-down and sad. Without him, it seemed desolate and creepy.

Normally Julie could have run up the stairs, grabbed the pictures and been back in the car in less than five minutes. But her ankle was starting to throb. She'd have to take it slow.

It surprised her that Candice had bothered with the pictures at all, but for some reason the woman really was trying to be helpful. She'd driven all the way to

Willow Creek Ranch to warn Julie about Troy's friend Able Drake.

Able wasn't an issue now that they knew Zeke Hartwell was the killer, but Candice hadn't known that then. As it turned out, Candice should have been the prime suspect, though no one knew that except her husband. He actually believed Candice had killed Muriel and yet he'd stayed with her.

What a strange marriage theirs must be.

Julie looked for any signs of life inside the house. She didn't want to encounter an addict getting high or coming down from one. The roaches, rats and scorpions would be company enough.

All was quiet and there was not another person in sight.

She got out of the car and made her way to the house. The door squeaked open. A breeze fluttered the old newspapers. Two huge rats sat on top of a window sill, so busily nibbling on an unidentifiable scrap they didn't bother to run away.

Julie started up the steps. Three steps from the top, she heard a clattering noise as if someone had fallen or bumped into a piece of furniture. Her heart jumped to her throat.

"Is anybody here?"

No one answered. She was letting her imagination get the best of her. First ghosts. Now noises.

The old floor creaked beneath her as she walked toward the desk. There was no sign of the pictures. But Julie was certain Candice had said she'd left them on the rolltop desk. If they weren't there, she'd give up and come back later. Her ankle felt like it was being pierced by a hundred tiny pins. Climbing stairs had aggravated it more than she'd expected.

Julie pulled a knob on one of the drawers. The whole thing came off in her hand. Okay, this was starting to get ridiculous. Now that she thought about it, she couldn't imagine Candice with her jewels and makeup even walking into this place.

This was some kind of sick trick they'd played on her. Sheriff Grayson might even be in on it. Him or Guy.

Joke over. She was out of here.

She swatted at a roach that started up her leg.

"Did you really think I'd give you pictures of your mother or Muriel?"

"Candice." Julie spun around and stared into the barrel of a shotgun.

"I liked you, Julie," Candice said. "I really did. I told Sheriff Grayson that when he said you were going to cause trouble for all of us. I liked you, but you just wouldn't leave well enough alone."

Zeke Hartwell was the murderer. Not Candice. None of this made sense. Nothing but the shotgun pointed at her head.

"I've quit the investigation, Candice. It's over. Zeke Hartwell is the murderer."

"Don't try to trick me, Julie. I know who killed Muriel. I've always known. So has Sheriff Grayson."

"That's not true. If the sheriff knew Zeke had killed Muriel, he would have arrested him."

"It wasn't Zeke. Stop saying that. And start walking, Julie. We have one more set of steps to climb."

"I can't climb anymore. I sprained my ankle, remember? It hurts too bad for me to climb."

"Climb the steps or I shoot you here."

Julie looked into Candice's cold black eyes and saw the evil Helene's ghost had warned her about. She had no doubt that Candice would kill her just as she said.

She didn't want to die. Not now. She wanted life. She wanted to feel joy and even pain. And she wanted to make love with Tyler.

Love was the sign.

She loved Tyler and she was sure they could make that love work. But first she had to get out of this house alive.

"Start walking or die."

Julie began to walk, the dread so overpowering she didn't feel her ankle at all.

"Who killed Muriel?" Julie asked, desperately trying to figure out what was going on in Candice's mind.

"Guy killed her, but it was her fault. She was having his baby and she wanted him to leave me."

"But why kill her?"

"It was the only way she'd ever let him go."

"Did he tell you that?"

"He didn't have to. I saw how upset he became when she died and I knew he hadn't wanted to do it. But he had to do it. It was the only way to get her and that baby out of our lives."

Julie kept climbing as the pieces began to fall into place. This was too bizarre, too unbelievably bizarre. Candice was convinced that Guy had killed Muriel. And Julie was almost positive that Guy thought Candice had committed the crime. They'd both lived under that assumption for years.

Living in the same house. Sleeping in the same bed. Sharing a marriage with someone you thought was a murderer.

The stress of it must have finally driven Candice completely mad.

Julie reached the top step. "Now what?"

"Now with a little help, you're going to fall out that rotting window. Like I said. The house is in terrible shape. Someone was bound to die here eventually."

SHERIFF GRAYSON WAS READY TO call it a day. It had been a long week what with having to deal with Julie Gillespie, but that was over and done and only a minimum amount of damage control had been necessary.

Zeke Hartman had been arrested for the murder of Muriel Frost, simply because he was too stupid to follow Grayson's advice. All he had to do was stick the envelope on Julie's windshield and then get out of Texas until things blew over. He couldn't even pull that off.

He'd have been arrested years ago if Grayson hadn't covered for him. Not that it hadn't been to Grayson's advantage. Zeke was mean as a snake and dumb as a toad. It had paid to have a man like that indebted to him.

Grayson's gravy train had officially run dry, but he'd never expected it to run this long. Neither Guy nor Candice could file charges against him without incriminating themselves. Guy had paid Grayson to keep his wife from going to jail for murdering Muriel. Candice had paid him for not jailing Guy for murder. It had been extremely profitable while it lasted, but now the game would simply come to an end.

Caleb Grayson, the winner by approximately $850,000. A rather neat little nest egg.

His cell phone rang. The ID said Guy Cameron. Grayson took the call. Might as well get this over with.

"I just got a call from Candice. She's at the farmhouse."

"The crime scene?"

"Yes, and you need to get over there fast."

"Why?

"She has Julie Gillespie. She says I'm going to be home free, whatever the hell that means. That's why I've got to get out there. Meet me at the farmhouse, Grayson. I'm on my way there now."

"Right. I'll meet you there."

A second later, Grayson was on the run. First stop the bank. Next stop, a quiet little island where he and his nest egg would never be found.

Two men in jeans and sport coats were waiting for him when he stepped out of the office.

"Hayden Gibbs, Texas Ranger."

"I can't stop to talk right now. I'm on an emergency call."

"Not anymore." The man who'd done all the talking produced a pair of handcuffs. "Zeke Hartwell has been spilling his guts all night. You're under arrest for obstruction of justice in the murder of Muriel Frost. And from what I hear, that's just for starters."

THERE WERE TWO CARS PARKED in front of the farm-house when Tyler arrived. One was Julie's. The other was the yellow Jaguar that Candice had driven to the ranch. No reason to panic, he told himself, but adrena-line rushed his bloodstream as he raced to the house.

The house was deathly quiet. If anyone was here, they must be in the attic. He raced up the steps. When he neared the top, he heard the sounds of splintering wood.

"One more board, Julie, and then you'll just tumble to your death."

Tyler crept to the opening that led to the half-rotted circle, all that was left of the crumbling attic. And then he saw Julie's reflection in the old floor mirror and panic gripped him with paralyzing force.

Candice held a shotgun just inches from Julie's head while Julie tore at the rotten wood window facing with her bare hands. The facing was so loose now that any pressure would send it careening out the opening to the ground three floors below.

One wrong move on his part and Candice might pull the trigger. If he waited, one shove from Candice could send Julie hurling to her death.

For one split second, he was back on the ranch and his mother was lying on the floor in a pool of her blood. He'd been helpless then. He wasn't now. He was a trained soldier. More than that, he was a man protecting the woman he loved.

Tyler watched a large scorpion crawl across the base-board, inching along, taking forever. But one more foot and it would be close enough he could reach it without Candice seeing him.

Candice took a step toward Julie. "You can stop now. The window is ready to fall."

Tyler grabbed the giant scorpion by the tail at the exact same instant that Julie jumped away from the window. The scorpion caught in Candice's bangs and dangled over her eyes. She screamed and waved her arms in frantic, erratic movements.

Her feet got tangled in the scraps of wood, and she fell toward the window. Tyler made a diving tackle and caught her a heartbeat before she fell.

"Nice tackle."

Tyler reached for Julie and pulled her into his arms just as two men in jeans and sport coats stepped into the attic with them.

"Hayden Gibbs, Texas Ranger."

"Tyler Ledger, cowboy/soldier, and I never thought I'd be so happy to see a ranger. How did you know to come?"

"A nice tip from Guy Cameron."

"Guy told you to save me?"

"That's Candice Cameron," Tyler said. "She was ready to push Julie out of the window and almost fell herself."

"Yeah, we caught the tail end of the action, but we weren't close enough to make the tackle."

"Where is Guy?" Candice asked.

"He's waiting on you—in jail. So is your friend Caleb Grayson."

"And you, Tyler, can take Julie home, unless she'd rather we drive her."

"I'll go with Tyler," she said.

"Somebody will be by tomorrow to ask a few questions, but right now I'd say Julie Gillespie deserves a warm bed and a pair of strong arms to comfort her."

Tyler would be more than happy to provide that—if she'd have him.

Julie took one step, and then winced in pain.

"We'd better call an ambulance," Hayden said.

"No need," Julie said. "Tyler knows exactly how to carry me."

Both rangers grinned. "Nice work, cowboy."

Tyler scooped her in his arms, carried her down three flights of stairs and placed her in the passenger seat of the car.

"Don't drive yet," she said, scooting into his arms. "Just hold me for a minute."

"I'll hold you for as long as you'll let me, Julie. A minute. A day. A lifetime."

"Is that a promise?"

"I kind of meant it as a proposal. Dylan needs a partner. I need a job, at least I will in a few months."

"What about Troy?"

"I don't expect miracles, but you were right about that, too. I'd convinced myself I didn't need him or my family. But in truth, it was my need to belong that brought me back to Texas. It's time I give him and Willow Creek Ranch a chance."

"No reenlisting?"

"No reenlisting. I'm glad I did my part for my country. But that's not the life for me."

"But..."

He kissed her silent. "I had all the time I needed to learn about love when I saw that shotgun pointed at your head tonight, Julie. I know we'll have some things to work out, but if you love me the way I love you, we can't miss."

"I love you with all my heart," she said. "And I know just where I want to get married."

"Anywhere you say."

"In that field of bluebonnets behind the ranch house."

"They won't bloom again for another year."

"Then we'll just have to get married before you leave."

Tyler kissed her again, knowing the wedding couldn't come too quickly for him. "I have one request, too," he said.

"Name it, cowboy."

"I want to see you wearing those shorts and cracking that whip on our honeymoon."

"Why wait? That's just the warm-up act."

Julie snuggled in Tyler's arms for one long last kiss before they started the drive home. The wedding would be in less than a week, but the lifetime of love was already beating in her heart.

When it's right, you get a sign. And the sign is love.

* * * * *

⬥™ Harlequin®

INTRIGUE®

COMING NEXT MONTH

Available April 12, 2011

REQUEST YOUR FREE BOOKS!
2 FREE NOVELS PLUS 2 FREE GIFTS!

Harlequin®

INTRIGUE®

BREATHTAKING ROMANTIC SUSPENSE

YES! Please send me 2 FREE Harlequin Intrigue® novels and my 2 FREE gifts (gifts are worth about $10). After receiving them, if I don't wish to receive any more books, I can return the shipping statement marked "cancel." If I don't cancel, I will receive 6 brand-new novels every month and be billed just $4.24 per book in the U.S. or $4.99 per book in Canada. That's a saving of at least 15% off the cover price! It's quite a bargain! Shipping and handling is just 50¢ per book in the U.S. and 75¢ per book in Canada.* I understand that accepting the 2 free books and gifts places me under no obligation to buy anything. I can always return a shipment and cancel at any time. Even if I never buy another book, the two free books and gifts are mine to keep forever.

182/382 HDN FC5H

Name	(PLEASE PRINT)	
Address		Apt. #
City	State/Prov.	Zip/Postal Code

Signature (if under 18, a parent or guardian must sign)

Mail to the **Reader Service:**
IN U.S.A.: P.O. Box 1867, Buffalo, NY 14240-1867
IN CANADA: P.O. Box 609, Fort Erie, Ontario L2A 5X3

Not valid for current subscribers to Harlequin Intrigue books.

**Are you a subscriber to Harlequin Intrigue books
and want to receive the larger-print edition?
Call 1-800-873-8635 or visit www.ReaderService.com.**

* Terms and prices subject to change without notice. Prices do not include applicable taxes. Sales tax applicable in N.Y. Canadian residents will be charged applicable taxes. Offer not valid in Quebec. This offer is limited to one order per household. All orders subject to credit approval. Credit or debit balances in a customer's account(s) may be offset by any other outstanding balance owed by or to the customer. Please allow 4 to 6 weeks for delivery. Offer available while quantities last.

Your Privacy—The Reader Service is committed to protecting your privacy. Our Privacy Policy is available online at www.ReaderService.com or upon request from the Reader Service.

We make a portion of our mailing list available to reputable third parties that offer products we believe may interest you. If you prefer that we not exchange your name with third parties, or if you wish to clarify or modify your communication preferences, please visit us at www.ReaderService.com/consumerchoice or write to us at Reader Service Preference Service, P.O. Box 9062, Buffalo, NY 14269. Include your complete name and address.

HII1

Selene wanted nothing to do with the father of her son, Alex; but Aristedes had other plans...that included them.

Read on for an sneak peek from
THE SARANTOS SECRET BABY by Olivia Gates,
available April 2011, only from Harlequin Desire.

"You were right to turn my marriage offer down," Aristedes said.

And Selene found her voice at last, found the words that would not betray the blow he'd dealt her. "Thanks for letting me know. You didn't have to come all the way here, though. You could have just let it go. I left yesterday with the understanding that this case is closed."

Before the hot needles behind her eyes could dissolve into an unforgivable display of stupidity and weakness, she began to close the door.

The door stopped against an immovable object. His flat palm.

"I can't accept that." His voice was low, leashed.

What did her tormentor mean now? Was he ending one game only to start another?

She raised eyes as bruised as her self-respect to his, found nothing there but solemnity and determination.

Before she could voice her confusion, he elaborated. "I never let anything go unless I'm certain it's unworkable. I realize I made you an unworkable offer, and that's why I'm withdrawing it. I'm here to offer something else. A workability study."

She leaned against the door, thankful for its support and partial shield. "Your son and I are not a business venture you can test for feasibility."

His gaze grew deeper, made her feel as if he was trying to delve into her mind, take control of it. "It's actually the other way around. I'm the one who would be tested."

She shook her head. "Why bother? I know—and *you* know—you're not workable. Not with me."

His spectacular eyebrows lowered over eyes she felt were emitting silver hypnosis. "You're right again. Neither you nor I have any reason to believe that isn't the truth. The only truth. It might be best for both you and Alex to never hear from me again, to forget I exist. But then again, maybe not. I'm only asking for the chance for both of us to find out for certain. You believe I'm unworkable in any personal relationship. I've lived my life based on that belief about myself. I never really had reason to question it. But I have one now. In fact, I have two."

Find out what happens in
THE SARANTOS SECRET BABY by Olivia Gates,
available April 2011, only from Harlequin Desire.

SDEXP0411